The Danc
Partner

The Dance Partner

DIANE GLANCY

Michigan State University Press
East Lansing

∞ The paper used in this publication meets the minimum requirements of ANSI/NISO Z39.48-1992 (R 1997) (Permanence of Paper).

Michigan State University Press
East Lansing, Michigan 48823-5245

Printed and bound in the United States of America.

11 10 09 08 07 06 05 1 2 3 4 5 6 7 8 9 10

Library of Congress Cataloging-in-Publication Data

Glancy, Diane.
The dance partner / Diane Glancy.
p. cm.
ISBN 0-87013-757-3 (pbk. : alk. paper)
1. Indians of North America—Fiction. 2. Ghost dance—Fiction.
I. Title.
PS3557.L294D36 2005
813'.54—dc22

200519499

Cover design by BookComp, Inc.
Book design by BookComp, Inc.

Cover artwork is The Ghost Dance by Oscar Howe (© 1983 Adelheid Howe, all rights reserved) and is used courtesy of Adelheid Howe and the Heard Museum, Phoenix, Arizona.

Michigan State University Press is a member of the Green Press Initiative and is committed to developing and encouraging ecologically responsible publishing practices. For more information about the Green Press Initiative and the use of recycled paper in book publishing, please visit www.greenpressinitiative.org.

Visit Michigan State University Press on the World Wide Web at:
www.msupress.msu.edu

We ran into another way of life and these shapes of writing are our stories after the collision.

I am memory, the destroyer of peace.
—Ronin of the Imperial Moat, *Hiroshima Bugi: Atomu 57,* by Gerald Vizenor

The universe had multiple histories.
—Richard Feynman

History also has multiple histories.
This is a part of America's history.

Contents

Preface

What is this but history that has been cut into and jumbled beyond what could be straightened out? Like Desoto's car when he hit a ditch at a hundred miles an hour. Some of these stories are stubs. Just stubs of stories. Sometimes mostly that's all we got.

I wanted to write a novel about the Ghost Dance, the late-nineteenth-century phenomenon among Native American tribes in the West that resulted in the belief that the white man would disappear and the old ways would return. There are existing historical texts of the Ghost Dance, but there are questions that have not been answered. Were the messianic dances an example of hysteria by a people whose way of life was coming to an end? Was it an *end time* happening, a cataclysmic close to tribal life on a continent that involved a deus ex machina? Was it a combination of several factors that ended in despondency, disillusionment, and the 1890 massacre at Wounded Knee? What exactly happened?

In these stories, I take the words of Native Americans such as Porcupine and Kicking Bear, along with the ethnologist James Mooney, and add imagined voices. Native American writing sometimes takes what is known and posits it alongside what could have been. In a culture where much has been erased or lost, the fragments of what is known are woven with the possibilities of what could have been. It is a technique called *ghosting*, which also is used at some historical sites in re-creating forts. It presents the image of what could have been, according to what is known of early architecture, or with descriptions or clues of some sort—though what actually existed is not known. *Ghosting* in writing presents a blueprint of voices that might have been, along with the structure of those voices that are known to have been.

Though the fragments of the 1870–1890 Ghost Dance are integral to the book, the novel would not stay centered in the Ghost Dance. It became a conglomerate of disparate pieces of historical journals, creative nonfiction, short fictional pieces, contemporized myths, and an augmented diary excerpt. *The Dance Partner* begins with a contemporary piece, then jumps back to the Ghost Dance and further back to the Sioux Uprising, and then forward again across 117 years of Plains Indian history. The novel depicts how history is not history, but reaches its *presence* into the present until the future is the past transformed. The dances to restore ancestors and animals and land in the face of the encroachment of the white man are still being reenacted in contemporary lives as Indians attempt to regain *life*. In fact, these stories are a Ghost Dance. They circle in the face of what *is* in relationship to what was and will be, with sharp fracture lines and disparities in story structure.

Indian thinking is nonlinear, non-chronological. The past roams into the present. A present-day story starts with the past. The past starts with the present. The spirits hitch-hike along the interstate. History comes down the road in a variety of vehicles, out of order, a carnival truck with different rides, setting up the unreality of a fun-house mirror, distorting what appears in it. The supernatural also is present. In *American Gypsy*, a collection of my plays, I write about native theory, calling the happenings *realized improbabilities* or *improbable realities.*

Once in a while I also use misappropriations of language, solecism, invented words, partial sentences, and phrase blocks to show how the old way of thinking seeps into English, the new language that has been learned.

The Ghost Dance is full of versions. It had been going on long before the white man came; it was a knowledge of loss and restoration that had nothing to do with Christianity. It was a result of the coming of the white man and the desperation that ensued. It was Christ appearing to the Indians. It was a contrivance by Mormons who lived nearby, especially the part about the appearance of Christ. It was something. It was nothing.

I wanted to conjure the jagged pieces of Plains Indian history. How history—a slice of it anyway, an unknown but significant part of it—took place in the geography of American history, however uncertain, whether a moment of truth (there is a beyond), a lie (there is nothing but trance induced by endless dancing), a conspiracy, a manipulation, a trick, a closeout that had ongoing effects. The Ghost Dance didn't end, but its apparition haunts subsequent years that seem different but are related—the same, actually—with transformation so complete the Ghost Dance no longer looks like the Ghost Dance. It is marked by its seeming absence. It carries the influence of the broken past to the broken present. There are trace elements of the dance in each story, and elements of history are in each contemporary life.

I also work with *story* as *shape* of Indian thinking. Fractured, fragmented, with invisible silences where further voices speak. There are stories within story, such as the Greek myth of Antiope *undershadowing* the story "Auntie Opey," and the rewrite or *overwrite* of the history of Richard Cardinal in "A Green Rag-Braided Rug" that gives him a life that he could have had with the right foster parents and opportunity. Cardinal also possibly could be involved in the first story, "The Dance Partner." Maybe sometimes it is something close to author intrusion but not quite. Time is referential and linear only in the sense of causal. The Ghost Dance was warped by what came before it, as it warped what came after it: the Hiawatha Asylum for Insane Indians and the contemporary sections that hold the separate fragments of these related stories in a circle of unresolved resolutions.

In the end, the Ghost Dance provided, and still provides, the possibility of a rewritten life.

The Dance Partner

2001

Between 1778 and 1871, there were 374 treaties. All of them broken. The people massacred. Dying of disease, starvation, disheartedness. From 1872 to 1874, three and a half million buffalo were slaughtered. What do you do when two people want the same land? What do you do with the defeated? The Indians did not disappear, as was hoped, but lived through their ice age. They endured the chill. The freezing. The ice cap on their heads. Their chairs placed on an ice block. Let them cipher zero. Let them figure there is no way to figure. Leave them alone in their despair.

The Indians called the white men *the-ones-who-sat-on-water* (came in boats). They were *the-ones-who-brought-their-strong-oarsmen*: smallpox, diphtheria, measles, cholera, tuberculosis, scarlet fever, influenza, diabetes.

They were *the-ones-who-brought-reservations-to-the-land.* The *can't-go-beyond*, the Indians called the land allotments.

They are writing now their history books. This is as it was remembered by the defeated. Not the ones glowing from within at their fire, their will imposed on men and animals and land. The Indians talked in secret. They talked in the dark. It would be theirs again. They didn't know how. But the white men would leave.

Meanwhile, the Indians were in a state of pupilage. They were wards of the state. They had been cheated. They had been duped. They had been defeated. They were closed off from what had been theirs. Their grandfathers and *their* grandfathers had migrated and hunted as they chose. Now there was another people telling them where to go and where to stay.

One day they would come back to destroy America's memory of itself. Uncover its history of robbery from the Indians. What could the Indians have done anyway?

The Dance Partner is their side of the story in this history they are writing, written in their own way.

The Indians prayed to the God the white men brought crumpled in a book: a stick man with outstretched arms. But it was the buffalo that died for the Indians. Why did they need this Christ? This mystery? This contradiction?

If they could have seen paradise, they might have understood their new dance partner, the pew and immovable altar, the *ranchero* of the Holy Ghost. But instead, they walked their canoes across ice.

Where is the way to Paradise? Did the Ghost Dancers ask? Faith in Christ? Believing he died for their sins?

They were poor and they were pitiful.

He was at the end of the road. He was at the last chance. He was beyond his last stand.

Don't you get tired of fighting? Don't you want to walk clean in the light of the living? the minister, the men in black robes asked.

They had to keep changing the stories because a story told more than once was too heavy to bear. A story told several times could weigh them down, even crush them. But they had to keep listening. Their survival was in what they heard. They kept hunting for stories so they could have different stories to tell. Their guns were ready, their game bags open. They only had to bag some words and they would live.

Their stories were a travois on which to carry the past. Stories couldn't be left behind. They were a part of them.

They couldn't be cut off like a leg or arm. Can anyone cut the spine out of a living body? That's what the past is. That's what stories are. They had to carry them as they moved on. No, the stories couldn't be cut off, but they could be lived with in a different way.

Most of the words for stories were gone from the plains. They had traveled beyond, following the Ghost Dancers, leaving an open suck-hole in their wake.

A woman coughed without stopping, but the meeting continued. He was late, but he came nonetheless. He had worked all day, he had eaten at his house, he had left his wife and children. If he wanted to survive for his family, he had to be here. The Holy Ghost asked him to dance. It was awkward. He went one way, the Holy Ghost another.

In the afterlife, they would need nothing. In the afterlife, they would be with the ancestors, the buffalo, the Maker. That is all they would want. They would not drink alcohol, nor commit suicide in other ways. Their dreams would be alive. Their dreams would lead them to their next camp. Their dreams would be the horses and pack dogs that carried their burdens. The afterlife was the next world into which this shadow world would roll. This shadow world was a dance to see who would roll.

He cried out for his family that was torn apart by poverty and want. He was drawn to the cross, to the awful Savior pelted by sin, worn away by disease, bitten into, hunks of flesh taken from him. In the awful darkness was salvation. The Savior carried his weight on the cross. He only had to believe.

He was drawn into the sky where he saw trails of Indians riding the plains of the universe. He saw the shelves of heaven made from all trees that ever lived. The forests of heaven. The swamp of darkness underneath him. The slag and slomp of everlasting dark. The heated dark. The roar sometimes of an old engine.

Christianity separated people from themselves. Jesus saved the individual. That is the way it was. They had to separate from their tribes. They had to stand before the Lord on their own. It was responsibility for one's self alone. If Christianity was true, what was it like to walk through the Milky Way to the afterworld? Even the children were on their own. He could not help his sons, his daughters, not even his wife. But he could show them the way by walking it himself. He thought of the judgment seat. Was that what it was called? It was frightening to think of. But God would be with him. Didn't the scriptures say? Maybe he could turn into a bear. Everyone turned up in the skins they hunted. A migration trail. How would they set up camp?

He thought of flying above the earth without a plane, seeing the earth puckered with erosion, darkened by trees, whitened with snow. He thought of the squared fields, the tar and creosote roads, the wrinkled valleys, the black hills. Then the bald fields of space with everyone waiting in line, like the airport now where federal agents waited when you came back from a foreign country or flew to another city. People moved all over the earth despite borders and barriers and security gates.

Who did Christ die for? Himself. Or rather, God. It was an agreement they had. God had to pour out his wrath. He chose his own son. He knew that one—beating his own son until his wife threw herself at him.

The prairie spread westward. There was nothing but land and sky and a few clumps of brush in the distance. Sometimes a slough or a few marsh grasses. In summer, maybe the peak of a bright yellow field—*kanola*, it was called. The sun gleaned the land, distant and unaware of the earth that received the light it gave, and then took back. The land was a wide road that sloped downward toward the rim of the earth.

The past came upon the gleam of the present, shuttered the edge of light, and banked into the room. He began to know something else was there.

Men had sinned, and God was all wrathful because he was a just God and could not bypass his need for justice. It was God's nature. Christ received that wrath on the cross. Then God was appeased forever. He just looked at men through Christ. Humanity was forgiven in Christ. The power of the resurrected Christ would help him stop drinking, would calm his rage.

The purpose of story was to congeal. Stories were told to hold the tribe together. When they were shut off, the stories still spoke. He knew them in his nightmares. He talked them in his sleep. In his dreams, he saw the ones running and shouting.

He remembered the massacres.

A nightmare could come through a keyhole.

This is ice you are walking on—underneath, the cold water that could drink you.

It is frightening. It is disquieting to have your luggage gone through. To be searched, scrutinized. They have the power to hold you back from where you want to go. And this, the final destination. The robe of the plane you are riding in—this time with tail winds pushing you along. The final judgment tables in the wind. Long lines. You can see beyond the checkpoint. It is where you want to go. The mountains and rivers and plains of heaven. Everything you wanted. What you've longed for those times alone when you opened before yourself and knew the intense loneliness and disappointment. The broken tribe. The drunk friends killed on dark roads. The white crosses that bloom like wildflowers. Or the times surrounded by family when you looked from the window a moment, just a moment, and knew you wanted to be someplace else. And all you need now is for your name to be in that book, and the page is turned just like at the polling booth—but no, this time your name isn't there, because you hadn't registered with Christ. You had ignored him all your life. The only ticket to enter the hereafter was Christ whom you ignored. How would you like that?

Ghost Dance

GHOST DANCE

He gave me a box wrapped with ribbon and paper.
There were buffalo inside the box, and the ancestors,
and a lake, and a teepee, and the earth as it was.

Now listen. There is something you may not want to hear. Then just close the book. But Jesus Christ came from the Maker to make our path through the world. In him, we who had nothing gained all things. He was seen in visions and dreams by the Indians. We were being pushed off the edge of the earth. He was there to meet us. When he appeared, some looked and saw no one. Others looked and saw a man with holes in his hands.

1888, Walker Lake, Nevada

We arrived half-mad from hunger. We arrived half-crazy from travel and the heat. We were sick. We were defeated. We were dying. We heard Wovoka was giving hope to the Indian people. We heard he was teaching the tribes to ghost-dance. We wanted to go. We wanted to see what was happening.

We had signed treaties. We had given up land. We were pushed aside until we could not move. A new world covered us with its heavy blanket. There was no place to step. Our feet felt tied together. The hungry cries of our children filled our ears. The boundaries of our reservation were not clear. Surveyors took a long time to tell us what was ours. Meanwhile, the whites kept moving in. We were not paid for our land. The rations of coffee, meat, flour were smaller than promised. If we gave up more land, our sacks would be full, they said. But our sacks were not full. Sometimes the rations were not there at all. Finally we heard the Ghost Dance was sweeping through the tribes to the west.

We rode four days from South Dakota to the end of the railroad tracks. Our women did not want us to go. They huddled together and cried. They were afraid we wouldn't return. They wanted to come to the station with us, but we had no horses. We were afraid for them to walk back without us.

The white children stared as we boarded. Their mothers pulled them away from us. People whispered. We sat by ourselves and said nothing. We held the dried bread our women wrapped in a cloth. The train made a harsh rattling noise as it traveled overland. It was faster than a horse, but it sent sparks and ashes into our faces. The seats were hard. Our backs hurt. We could not sleep sitting up. We could not lie down. We passed mountains we had not seen before. We were stiff and dazed as we looked at one another without speaking.

We felt like we were still on the train when we disembarked. We rode another four days on horseback to Walker Lake, Nevada. At night, the land passed as if it was still moving. We dreamed of our hungry women and children. We dreamed as if we were awake. Each night, someone came to the camp. He had a blue wagon with springs that did not jolt over the ground. In the wagon, he had a trunk and some bundles. He said he had magic to make treaties go away. He said he had animals with fur that we could hunt, if we stayed with him. But we had a bad feeling about the man, and each morning we decided to ride on.

After four days, we arrived at a strange camp of brush arbors and wickiups made of rush. The land was desert surrounded by mountains. Small clumps of sagebrush covered the land. The desert floor was sandy dirt with grainy pebbles. We felt it under our moccasins. We felt it under our blankets on the dirt floor of the wickiup open to the sky. At first we lay on the ground looking up into the air. After they gave us water and seed mush and piñon nuts, we began to recover.

When I could sleep, I dreamed of my old wife wrapped in a torn blanket. There was a tattered cloud above her in the sky. I felt a stab of pain because I had to leave her. She wouldn't look at me, but kept her head down. I went away as if I didn't notice. The women had made their tremolo as we left, but we would return.

When a new world comes, it drives out the old one. The Indian was the old world on its way out. We saw the killing of buffalo. The arrival of wagon trains. The settlers. The railroad. Our removal to reservations. But it was more than that. We felt the war in the spirit world above us. It was hard to tell what was going on. The spirits were of opposite camps, yet they could seem almost the same.

We were disappointed. We were discouraged. Our thoughts opened to hopelessness. We knew the whites were coming. We felt them before we saw the trail of their wagons, their forts, their homesteads scattered on the land. But the visions and prophecies also kept coming. The new world would disappear. The old world would return. When was it coming? Some said they saw nothing when they danced. Others saw the other world. Is that the way then? In a thought?

At first we sat in the arbors on the edge of the dance. We listened to Wovoka, a Paiute. Then we danced a dance which was not much more than moving our feet. We circled and circled. Some began to fall on the ground as though they were asleep. I felt my head grow light. I saw into another world. It was, at first, blurred as if far away—then slowly it came into focus, into recognition. In the visions, we went to a far land. There always was someone trying to keep us from going. Promising war horses and whatever we needed. But we followed the path through a haze or fog into the vision. There was the Great Spirit, his wife, and many people in the place beyond. They were fishing and hunting on a wide plain. I felt my eyes sting. I had to look away. My eyes hurt just like my jaw when I took a bite of seed mush in the wickiup when I was hungry. It was tears that throbbed in my eyes. I had to shut them because they hurt. I swallowed. I had to remember bravery. My legs were weak. I couldn't tell who the people in the vision were. They remained blurry. I couldn't see as yet. Maybe I would have seen too much. But I heard what others said when we came back from the trance. Someone on the edge of camp quieted a small group of horses. I wondered if they knew our visions. The message was, if you believed, you would see the ancestors again.

There was the old world and the new white world. There was the Great Spirit's world, the next world, and the Ghost Dance world, of which our visions were an edge. How many worlds were there?

One man said he saw his father on his way back to this world. When his father died, his mother gashed her arms. He and his brothers shot their ponies to show they suffered. They thought they would never see their father again. It was how they showed grief. Otherwise the loss was too heavy. But in the man's dream, he saw his father on his way back to this world.

Don't come, we wanted to say. We didn't want him to see what had happened on the earth.

Messages. Visions. Prophesies. Words. The air was full of them, and yet the white man came. We didn't know what to do. *Don't fight*, the visions said. Don't fight? Just stand there and let the new world come? Just stand there and let everything be taken from us? Just let our anger pound us? We waited for the white people to go. But more of them came.

Do not hurt anyone, the prophesies said. But weren't we hurt? *Do not tell lies.* Didn't they lie? They brought their world they could inhabit, but could we? They did not want us. We did not want them. There was no way to come together.

The visions forbade war. But if we could, we would have ridden our horses into battle. We would do anything to drive out the white man. The Ghost Dance tamed our people. We thought less of war and more of the next world. Some of us were healed by touching the world we saw in a vision. A fire would sweep the land and drive out the whites. The Indians would jump over the fire. Or the waters would come and rush into the mouths of the white men and choke them. The Indians, however, would climb over the waves.

Maybe we were the ghosts who danced, and in the dance, we saw *the real world* above us. We were the ghosts who danced, and in the dance we saw the spirit world. Sometimes the other world seemed to fade. Maybe the Great Spirit thought it wasn't time yet for the other world to return. It would be in the Great Spirit's time. Yes. We couldn't make it happen. It might take him a while to return the ghosts.

We wouldn't have known about Wovoka if it hadn't been for the Indian postmasters who had been to school. It was the educated Indians who wrote and read letters about Wovoka and the Ghost Dance. Wovoka was a Paiute who called himself a prophet. We wanted to hear Wovoka. We wanted to go to see what was happening. We felt the need to dance. We knew we weren't the only ones. We knew the dance was true because it happened in other places.

Christ would be there in two days, someone said. On the train? In a circus ring?

Someone else said smoke had descended on a house, and there stood Christ. Who was this Christ, this Messiah, who let his people kill him? Who was this God? Was he the Great Spirit? Was there God and the Great Spirit, Christ and the Messiah? And who was Wovoka? No, the Messiah the people talked about was not Wovoka, though some thought he was. Wovoka himself said he was not the Messiah, but a messiah, a prophet who brought a message.

Some of the people said the Messiah told them to kill a buffalo, leave its head and feet on the prairie, and the buffalo would come back alive. *Who said it?* we asked. *The Messiah or the messiah? The Messiah, likely*, they said. Yes, if they could find a buffalo. Other people said they had found a small herd of buffalo, killed one, left the head, feet, and tail behind. When they looked back, at some distance, they saw the buffalo again. That is the way the Messiah worked. Did it mean the dead soldiers we left on the prairie would return? We hoped not. For us, the buffalo didn't return. In the thunder, we heard the Buffalo Dance. Were they running from the next world? No—for us, they were running to it.

I will shorten your journey, the Great Spirit said. Some people said, *When we felt tired we slept, and found ourselves at a great distance.* But for others, the journey was long.

Water will destroy the whites, choking on waves in their mouths. Or fire. Or maybe a cyclone or whirlwind would suck them up. *But you will fly above it*, they said. *If you have feathers in your hair, your hair will lift you.*

We were weary. We were sad. We could not understand the confusion. In one vision, there was smoke from a forest fire. Who was there? God the Great Spirit, or Christ the Messiah, or Wovoka the prophet—what could we make of them? We danced. We ate piñon nuts and seed mush, sometimes small game and fish. We slept. We danced.

There was a long pole with an eagle feather tied to it. If anyone could climb the pole and put his mouth on the feather, he would see his dead mother. One man climbed the pole, fell back to the ground. They thought he was dead, but he recovered and said he had seen his mother and others. They were on their way back. Yes, that's what they all said. Had any of the dead shown up?

Another man thought of his father and brother. He saw them when they were young. Not children. But not old, he meant. They were coming back with the deer, antelope, buffalo. Maybe the ancestors would become a moose herd and return to us. *No, don't come back*, we wanted to tell them again.

We danced in a circle until our feet were suspended and we walked on air, changing as the clouds changed. Only here there were no clouds. In my trance, I stepped onto a large field, checked like my wife's old blanket—each square traveled across the sky as if a star. The whole sky was her blanket. I passed all the ages that were and would be. They rose from the blanket like balls of dust on fire.

The trances came from hunger. They came from need. They came from desperation. They came from the need to manipulate circumstances. To see beyond them. We sat in brush shelters and listened to Wovoka, whose names also were Cutter, Jack Wilson, and Kwohitsauq or Big Rumbling Belly. We danced in a circle until we fell. During the visions, we lay on the ground or slumped forward. We were desperate. We were frantic. The ground would swallow our enemies. People who died many years ago were seen. Chasing Hawk and his wife were sitting in their teepee in the next world. Other relatives were seen.

The Ghost Dance was widespread: Paiute, Bannock, Shoshoni, Arapaho, Cheyenne, Omaha, Winnebago, Dakota. It was in Nevada, Oregon, Utah, Idaho. We would take it back to South Dakota.

S. Selwyn, the postmaster at Pine Ridge, a Yankton Sioux, was the one who read the letters that came to us from other places. It is why we traveled to Walker Lake in Nevada. The postmaster could read the letters and tell us what they said. We knew what was going on in other places. We knew it was everywhere. Animals talked during that time. They were ghost-dancing too. Distant objects appeared close. Everything was distorted.

I had more dreams of my wife wrapped in her old checked blanket. The air above her was troubled by dreams.

They floated like clouds shaped by wind. Sometimes the Ghost Dance seemed to fade. There was the thought it was an image without meaning. We felt panic at the thought. We kept dancing.

On the reservation, there was starvation. There was measles. Grippe. Whooping cough. Sullenness and gloom. Our horses were taken. Our war ponies were removed. We were given stock, wagons, plows, and hoes. We were supposed to farm. But our crops failed. We didn't like living separate from one another. Our rations were insufficient. Our supplies disappeared. Winter clothing came midwinter. We killed our cattle to eat. We killed the cattle of the whites so that we wouldn't starve. After crop failure, the whites moved on. We had nowhere to go. Our children were hungry. Our hearts angry. There was drought. Hopelessness. Where did they expect us to turn? What did they expect us to do? We had problems with people changing at the agency. Each one had to learn from the beginning. There was no continuity.

We were disoriented. We were afraid. We were going different ways at once.

Father Jutz at the Drexel Mission in South Dakota fought a battle himself. He had talked of Peter's vision: the animals and birds let down from the sky in a blanket tied at the corner. His God told Peter he could eat all things [Acts 10:9–16]. But the bundle in our vision was carnage. Our own carnage. The carnage of our people. How do we live with disappointment? Or maybe not understanding what was happening? Still, the father talked of Peter's vision. But we could not eat tainted meat. We could not eat rations that were not there.

They came in regiments—the armies of the government. Then came the armies of God. There were fewer of them. Men in black robes who built square churches with steeples they said reached the sky. Then the black pelicans—women who taught in the square buildings they built beside the square church. Where did they get the shape of their buildings? How could we send our children there? Did they see anything square like that on the land? Did the Great Spirit build anything square? Did the animals? That's why the horses were restless in their corrals. They felt the square shape too. They were out of place. Sometimes the white man sent our children far away to school. We didn't see them for several years. They came back to us strangers.

How could we know the white man's God? Even he didn't know him.

There was a doctrine of the Mormons, whom Father Jutz was against. They preached the return of Christ, but it was not the true Christ. Father Jutz warned us. It might happen in the west. We had to beware. How were we to know? We were drawn to this Christ. Certainly he preached good things.

Jesus was a carpenter. He knew what would happen. When he hammered, did he think of the nails in his hand?

He liked the defeated. He liked the people who were driven from the earth. The Ghost Dance was outside us. It was something other than us. It had started with a man named Tavibo, who went up into the mountains like the white man's prophets. The good father would approve of that. Tavibo came back with messages. After Tavibo came Wovoka.

Jesus came from country like this. He liked the desert and mountains. He liked the water.

There were large birds at Walker Lake—pelicans, or some other bird. We didn't know the name.

Jesus came to us like a pelican on Walker Lake. He liked the lake. Yes, but he was looking for the sea. Here the sea was dry land. Jesus liked the contradiction. He liked to see what wasn't there. His friends were fishermen. But he was a carpenter. What could he do in the desert without trees? Build more wickiups made from tule rush?

White clouds arrived like large white birds. Jesus was a winged man. There would be a day when we could go where we wanted.

Did he come to the buffalo, who were the earth?

At night I could hear the spirits walking. Bumping into others sometimes in the dark.

What happened in Nevada? The trances, the hypnotic states—were they from something they gave us to eat [peyote]? Were they Mormon visions? Were they visions from the Great Spirit? Sometimes the news changed as it spread: there were two men or beings in white skins [Tavibo, the prophet before Wovoka, meant "white man"]. How could we know? Was the Ghost Dance a promise without substance? A promise made worse by its emptiness? Made the opposite of what it was? Hopelessness without hope of change—without relief for our anxiety—but complete and immovable in itself. Or did something real happen, threaded among the illusions?

Then we returned to South Dakota, saying farewell to those we would not see again—on this side of the world anyway. We rode four days on horseback. Four days on the train. Our women were waiting for us in their tattered blankets, crying, the same as when we left.

On the train, we had sat together, away from everyone else who stared at us. We were a pitiful people who had nothing. That's why we stood far back. That's why we didn't let them near. That's why we were silent if they came near. They would see we were nothing. They would know who we were.

The ancestors had been above us, yes, but not to return. No, I knew it then. They had come to take us where they were.

PORCUPINE TO MAJOR CARROLL, CAMP CROOK, TONGUE RIVER AGENCY, MONTANA, JUNE 15, 1890

I went to the agency at Walker Lake, and they told us Christ would be there in two days. At the end of two days, on the third morning, hundreds of people gathered at this place. They cleared off a place near the agency in the form of a circus ring, and we all gathered there. We waited there till late in the evening, anxious to see Christ. Just before sundown I saw a great many people, mostly Indians, coming dressed in white men's clothes. The Christ was with them. They all formed in this ring in a circle around him. They put up sheets all around the circle, as they didn't have tents. Just after dark some of the Indians told me that Christ was arrived. I looked around to find him, and finally saw him sitting on one side of the ring. They all started toward him to see him. They made a big fire to throw light on him. I never looked around, but went forward, and when I saw him I bent my head. I had always thought the Great Father was a white man, but this man looked like an Indian. He sat there a long time and nobody went up to speak to him. He sat with his head bowed all the time. After awhile he rose and said he was very glad to see his children. I have sent for you and am glad to see you. I am going to talk to you after a while about your relatives who are dead and gone. My children, I want you to listen to all I have to say to you. I will teach you, too, how to dance a dance, and I want you to dance it. Get ready for your dance, and when the dance is over I will talk to you. He was dressed in a white coat with stripes. The rest of his dress was a white man's, except that he had on a pair of moccasins. Then he commenced our dance, everybody joining in, the Christ singing while we danced. We danced till late in the night; then he told us we had danced enough.

The next morning, after breakfast was over, we went into the circle and spread canvas over it on the ground, the Christ standing in the midst of us. He told us he was going away that day, but would be back the next morning to talk to us.

In the night when I first saw him I thought he was an Indian, but the next day when I could see better he looked different. He was not so dark as an Indian, nor so light as a white man. He had no beard or whiskers, but had heavy eyebrows. He was a good-looking man. We were crowded up very close. We had been told that nobody was to talk, and that even if we whispered the Christ would know it. I had heard that Christ had been crucified, and I looked to see, and I saw a scar on his wrist and one on his face, and he seemed to be the man. He would talk to us all day.

That evening we assembled again to see him depart. When we were assembled he began to sing, and he commenced to tremble all over violently for a while and then sat down. We danced all the night, the Christ lying down beside us apparently dead.

The next morning when we went to eat breakfast, the Christ was with us. After breakfast four men went around and called out that the Christ was back with us and wanted to talk with us. The circle was prepared again. The people assembled, and Christ came among us and sat down. He said he wanted to talk to us again and us to listen. He said, *I am the man who made everything you see around you. I am not lying to you, my children. I made this earth and everything on it. I have been to heaven and seen your dead friends and have seen my own mother and father. In the beginning, after God made the earth, they sent me back to teach the people, and when I came back to the earth they were afraid of me and treated me badly. This is what they did to me* [showing his scars]. *I did not try to defend myself. I found my children were bad, so went back to heaven and left them. I told them that in so many hundred years I would come back to try to teach them. My father told me the earth was getting bad, and that I was to renew everything as it used to be, and make it better.*

He told us all our dead were to be resurrected; that they were all to come back to earth, and that as the earth was too small for them, he would do away with heaven and make the earth itself large enough to contain us all; that we must tell all the people we meet about these things. He spoke to us about fighting, and said that it was bad, and we must keep from it; that the earth was to be all good hereafter, and we must all be friends with one another. He said that in the fall of the year, the youth of all the good people would be renewed, so that nobody would be more than forty years old, and that if they behaved themselves well after this, the youth of everyone would be renewed in the spring. He said if we were all good, he would send people among us who could heal all our wounds and sickness by mere touch, and that we would live forever. He told us not to quarrel or fight, nor strike each other, nor shoot one another; that the whites and Indians were to be all one people. He said if any man disobeyed what he ordered, his tribe would be wiped from the face of the earth; that we must believe everything he said, and that we must not doubt him, or say he lied; that if we did, he would know it; that he would know our thoughts and actions, in whatever part of the world we might be.

When I heard this from the Christ, and came back home to tell it to my people, I thought they would listen. When I went [there], there were lots of white people, but I never had one of them say an unkind word to me. I thought all your people knew of this I have told you of, but it seems you did not.

Ever since Christ talked to me, I have thought what he said was good. I see nothing bad in it. When I got back, I knew my people were bad, and had heard nothing of all this, so I got them together and told them of it and warned them to listen to it for their own good. I talked to them for four nights and five days. I told them just what I have told you here today. I told them what I said were the words of God Almighty, who was looking down on them. I wish some of you had been up in our camp here to have heard my words to the Cheyenne. The only bad thing that there was in it at all was this: I had just told my people that Christ would visit the sins of any Indian upon the whole tribe, when the recent trouble [killing of Ferguson] occurred. If any one of you think I am not telling the truth, you can go and see this man I speak of for yourselves. I will go with you, and I would like one or two of my people who doubt me to go with me.

The Christ talked to us in our respective tongues. You can see this man in your sleep any time you want after you have seen him and shaken hands with him once. Through him you can go to heaven and meet your friends. Since my return, I have seen him often in my sleep. About the time the soldiers went up the Rosebud, I was lying in my lodge asleep when this man appeared and told me that the Indians had gotten into trouble, and I was frightened. The next night he appeared to me and told me that everything would come out all right.

KICKING BEAR, 1890

My brothers, I bring to you the promise of a day in which there will be no white man to lay his hands on the bridle of the Indian's horse; when the red men of the prairie will rule the world and will not be turned away from the hunting grounds any more. I bring you word from your fathers the ghosts, that they are now marching to join you, led by the Messiah who came once to live on the earth with the white men, but was cast out and killed by them. I have seen wonders of the spirit-land, and have talked with the ghosts. I traveled far and am sent back with a message to tell you to make ready for the coming of the Messiah and return of ghosts in the spring.

In my teepee on the Cheyenne Reservation, I rose after the corn planting, sixteen moons ago, and prepared for my journey. I had seen many things and had been told by a voice to go and meet the ghosts, for they were to return to inhabit the earth. I traveled far on the cars of the white men, until I came to the place the railroad stopped. There I met two men, Indians, whom I had never seen before, but who greeted me as a brother and gave me meat and bread. They had three horses, and we rode without talking for four days, for I knew they were to be witnesses to what I should see. Two suns we traveled, and had passed the last signs of the white man—for no white man had ever had the courage to travel so far—when we saw a strange and fierce-looking black man, dressed in skins. He was living alone, and had medicine with which he could do what he wished. He would wave his hands and make great heaps of money; another motion, and we saw many spring wagons, already painted and ready to hitch horses to; yet another motion of the hands, and there sprung before us great herds of buffalo. The black man spoke and told us that he was the friend of the Indian; that we should remain with him and go no farther, and we might take what we wanted of the money, and spring wagons, and the buffalo. But our hearts turned away from the black man, and we left him and traveled for two days more.

On the evening of the fourth day, when we were weak and faint from our journey, we looked for a camping place, and were met by a man dressed like an Indian, whose hair was long and glistening like the yellow money of the white man. His face was very beautiful to see, and when he spoke my heart was glad, and I forgot my hunger and the toil I had gone through. And he said, "How, my children. You have done well to make this long journey to come to me. Leave your horses and follow me." And our hearts sang in our breasts and we were glad. He led the way up a great ladder of small clouds, and we followed him up through an opening in the sky. My brothers, the tongue of Kicking Bear is straight and he cannot tell what he saw, for he is not an orator, but the forerunner and herald of the ghosts. He whom we followed took us to the Great Spirit and his wife, and we lay prostrate on the ground, but I saw that they were dressed like Indians. Then from an opening in the sky we were shown all the countries of the earth and the camping grounds of our fathers since the beginning; all were there, the teepees, and the ghosts of our fathers, and great herds of buffalo, and a country that smiled because it was rich and the white man was not there. Then he whom we had followed showed us his hands and feet, and there were wounds in them which had been made by the whites when he went to them and they crucified him. And he told us he was going to come again on the earth, and this time he would remain and live with the Indians, who were his chosen people.

Then we were seated on rich skins, of animals unknown to me, before the open door of the teepee of the Great Spirits, and he told us how to say the prayers and perform the dances I am now come to show my brothers. And the Great Spirit spoke to us saying:

Take this message to my red children and tell it to them as I say it. I have neglected the Indians for many moons, but I will make them my people now if they obey me in this message. The earth is getting old, and I will make it new for my chosen people, the Indians, who are to inhabit it, and among them will be all of their ancestors who have died, their fathers, mothers, brothers, cousins and wives—all those who hear my voice and my words through the tongues of my children.

I will cover the earth with new soil to a depth of five times the height of a man, and under this new soil will be buried all the whites, and all the holes and the rotten places will be filled up. The new lands will be covered with sweet-grass and running water and trees, and herds of buffalo and ponies will stray over it, that my red children may eat and drink, sing and rejoice. And the sea to the west I will fill up so that no ships may pass over it, and the other seas will I make impassable. And while I am making the new earth, the Indians who have heard this message and who dance and pray and believe will be taken up in the air and suspended there, while the wave of new earth is passing; then set down among the ghosts of their ancestors, relatives, and friends. Those of my children who doubt will be left in undesirable places, where they will be lost and wander around until they believe and leave the songs and the dance of the ghosts.

And while my children are dancing and making ready to join the ghosts, they shall have no fear of the white man, for I will take from the white man the secret of making gunpowder, and the powder they now have on hand will not burn when it is directed against the red people, my children, who know the songs and dances of the ghosts; but that powder which my children, the red men, have will burn and kill when it is directed against

> the whites and used by those who believe. And if a red man die at the hands of the whites while he is dancing, his spirit will only go to the end of the earth and there join the ghosts of his father and return to his friends in the spring. Go then, my children, and tell these things to all the people and make all ready for the coming of the ghosts.

We were given food rich and sweet to taste, and as we sat there eating, there came up through the clouds a man, tall as a tree and thin as a snake, with great teeth sticking out of his mouth, his body covered with short hair, and we knew at once it was an Evil Spirit. And he said to the Great Spirit, "I want half the people of the earth." And the Great Spirit answered and said, "No, I cannot give you any; I love them all too much." The Evil Spirit asked again and was again refused, and asked the third time, and the Great Spirit told him that he could have the whites to do what he liked with, but that he would not let him have any Indians, as they were his chosen people for all future time. Then we were shown dances and taught the songs that I am bringing you, my brothers, and we were led down the ladder of clouds by him who had taken us up. We found our horses and rode back to the railroad, the Messiah flying along in the air with us and teaching us the songs for the new dances. At the railroad, he left and told us to return to our people, and tell them, and all the people of the red nations, what we had seen; and he promised us that he would return to the clouds no more, but would remain at the end of the earth and lead the ghosts of our fathers to meet us when the next winter is passed.

JAMES MOONEY (WASICHU), ETHNOLOGIST FOR THE BUREAU OF AMERICAN ETHNOLOGY, 1890, NEVADA

I learned that the messiah lived not on the reservation, but in Mason valley, about 40 miles to the northwest. His uncle, Charley Sheep, lived near the agency. As usual, he was suspicious at first, but I told him I was sent by the government to various tribes to study their customs and learn their stories and songs; that I had obtained a good deal from other tribes and now wanted to learn some songs and stories of the Paiute, in order to write them down so the white people could read them. In a casual way I then offered to show him the pictures of some of my Indian friends across the mountains, and brought out the photos of several Arapaho and Cheyenne who I knew had recently come as delegates to the messiah. This convinced him I was all right, and he became communicative. The result was that we spent about a week together in the wickiups [lodges of tule rushes], surrounded by a crowd of Paiute, discussing the old stories and games, singing Paiute songs, and eating seed mush and roasted piñon nuts. On one of these occasions, at night, a medicine man was performing his incantations over a sick child on one side of the fire while we talked on the other. I cautiously approached the subject of the ghost songs and dance, and found no difficulty in obtaining a number of the songs, with a description of the ceremonial. I then told Charley I was anxious to see the messiah and get from him some medicine-paint to bring back to his friends among the eastern tribes. He readily agreed.

It was 20 miles northward by railroad from Walker River agency to Wabuska, and 12 miles southwest to the Mason valley settlement. There we met a young white man named Dyer, who was acquainted with Jack Wilson, and who also spoke the Paiute language, and learned from him that the messiah was about 12 miles farther up the valley, near a place called Pine Grove. Enlisting his services, with a team and a driver, making four in all, we started up toward the mountain. It was New Year's Day, 1892, and there was a deep snow on the ground, an unusual thing in this part of the country, and due in this instance, as Charley assured us, to the direct agency of Jack Wilson. It is hard to image anything more monotonously unattractive than a sage prairie under ordinary circumstances unless it be the same prairie when covered by a heavy fall of snow, under which the smaller clumps of sagebrush look like prairie-dog mounds, while the larger ones could hardly be distinguished at a short distance from wickiups.

Soon after leaving the settlement we passed the dance ground with the brush shelters still standing. We met but few Indians on the way. After several miles we noticed a man at some distance from the road with a gun on his shoulder. Dyer looked a moment and then exclaimed, "I believe that's Jack now!" The Indian thought so, too, and pulling up our horses he shouted some words in the Paiute language. The man replied, and sure enough it was the messiah, hunting jack rabbits.

As he approached I saw he was a young man, a dark full-blood. He was well dressed in white man's clothes, with the broad-brimmed white felt hat common in the west, secured on his head with a beaded ribbon under the chin. This, with a blanket or a robe of rabbit skins, was now the ordinary Paiute dress. He wore a good pair of boots. His hair was cut off square on a line below the base of the ears, in the manner of his tribe.

As he came up and took my hand with a hearty grasp, he inquired what was wanted. His uncle explained matters. After some deliberation he said that the whites had lied about him and he did not like to talk to them; but as I was sent by Washington and was a friend of his friends, he would talk with me. He was hunting now, but if we would come to his camp that night he would tell us about his mission.

With another hand-shake he left us, and we drove to the nearest ranch, arriving after dark. After supper we got ready and started across country through the sagebrush for the Paiute camp, some miles away, guided by our Indian. It was already night, with nothing to be seen but the clumps of snow-covered sagebrush stretching away in every direction, and after traveling an hour or more without reaching the camp, our guide had to confess that he had lost the trail. It was two years since he had been there, his sight was failing, and with the snow and darkness, he was at a loss to know his whereabouts.

There was no road, and no house but the one we had left some miles behind, and it would be nearly impossible to find our way back through the darkness. Except for a lantern there was no light but what came from the glare of the snow and a few stars in the frosty sky overhead. To add to our difficulty, the snow was cut in every direction by cattle trails, which seemed to be Indian trails, and kept us doubling and circling to no purpose, while in the uncertain gloom every large clump of sagebrush took on the appearance of a wickiup. With it all, the night was bitterly cold and we were half frozen. After vainly following a dozen false trails and shouting repeatedly, we hit on the expedient of leaving the Indian with the wagon, he being the oldest man of the party, while the rest of us took a different direction from the central point, following the cattle tracks in the snow and calling to each other at short intervals. After going far enough to know that none of us had yet struck the right trail, the wagon was moved up a short distance and the same performance was repeated. At last a shout from our driver brought us all together. He declared that he had heard sounds in front, and after listening, he saw a shower of sparks go up into the darkness and he knew that we had struck camp. Going back to the wagon, we got in and drove straight across to the spot, where we found three or four wickiups, in one of which we were told the messiah was waiting our arrival.

Wovoka received us cordially then inquired more particularly as to my purpose. His uncle entered into a detailed explanation, which stretched out to a preposterous length, owing to a peculiar conversational method of the Paiute. Each statement by the older man was repeated at its close, word for word and sentence by sentence, by the other, with the same monotonous inflection.

At last he signified that he understood and was satisfied, and then in answer to my questions gave an account of himself and his doctrine.

He had given the dance to his people about four years before, but had received his revelation about two years previously. On this occasion "the sun died" [was eclipsed] and he fell asleep and was taken to the other world. Here he saw God, with all the people who had died long ago. God told him he must go back and tell his people to work and not steal; that they could not war, and they would be reunited with their friends in this other world. He was then given the dance to bring back to his people. God also gave him control over the elements so that he could make it rain or snow or be dry at will, and appointed him deputy to take charge over matters in the west. He also said he believed it was better for the Indians to follow the white man's road and to adopt the habits of civilization.

From his uncle I learned that Wovoka has five songs for making it rain, the first of which brings on a mist or cloud, the second a snowfall, the third a shower, and the fourth a hard rain or storm, while the fifth song brings clear weather again.

He made no claim to be Christ, the Son of God, as had been often asserted in print. He did claim to be a prophet who had received divine revelation.

I learned that Wovoka had once requested a letter sent to the President with a proposition that if he could receive a small regular stipend he would take up his residence on the reservation and agree to keep Nevada informed of all the news from heaven and to furnish rain whenever wanted.

THE MESSIAH LETTER

When you get home you make dance, and will give you the same. when you dance four days and in night one day, dance day time, five days and then fifth, will wash five for every body. He likes you you give him good many things, he heart been satting feel good. After you get home, will give good cloud, and give you chance to make you feel good. and he give you good spirit. and he give you a good paint.

You folks want you come in three [months] here, any tribes from there. There will be good bit snow this year. Sometime rain's, in fall, this year some rain, never give you any thing like that. grandfather said when he die never cry, no hurt anybody. no fight, good behave always, it will give you satisfaction, this young man, he is a good Father and mother, dont tell no white man. Jusus was on ground, he just like cloud. Every body is alive again, I dont know when they will [be] here, maybe be this fall or in spring.

Every body never get sick, be young again—[if young fellow no sick any more], work for white men never trouble with him until you leave, then it shake the earth dont be afraid no harm any body.

You make dance for six weeks night, and put you foot [food?] in dance to eat for every body and wash in the water. this is all to tell, I am in to you. and you will received a good words from him stome time, Dont tell lie.

AMERICAN HORSE

Every year they cut our rations, and we do not get enough to keep us from suffering—bacon, beans, baking powder, beef, coffee, corn, flour, hard bread, mess pork, sugar, salt, soap. We see them disappear like water in a shallow slough in summer.

Cattle broke into our fields and trampled the crops—there was not time before winter to plant again. How many times are we brought to nothing? What will we do with our hunger? What do we do with our anger?

In the Ghost Dances we saw the sun, the moon, and stars. We saw buffalo, deer, antelope, rabbit, bear, wolf, puma. We saw eagle feathers and small cedar trees.

In our hands, we saw our desperation.

THE SAGE HEN

At first the world was covered with water. Then the water began to recede and at last Kurangwa [Mount Grant] emerged from the water, near the southwest end of Walker Lake. Afterwards, there was a fire on top of the mountain, and when the wind blew hard, the water spilled back over the mountain and would have put the fire out, but the sage hen nestled down over the top of the mountain and fanned away the water with her wings. The heat scorched the feathers on her breast and that's why the feathers of the sage hen remain black to this day.

The Ghost Dance at Wounded Knee

Rosebud, 1890s

I was born before the census taker and I don't know how old I am. But when I was a young boy, I liked to be with my uncle because he told stories. "There's something new coming, traveling in the wind. A new dance. A new prayer." He was talking about the *wanagi-wachipi,* the Ghost Dance. "Short Bull and Kicking Bear went to see a Paiute holy man [in Nevada]. They had heard this holy man could bring dead people to life again, and that he could bring the buffalo back." My uncle said I should listen closely.

This holy man let Short Bull and Kicking Bear look into his hat. There they saw their dead relatives walking around. The holy man told them, "I'll give you something to eat that will kill you, but don't be afraid. I'll bring you back to life again." They believed him. They ate something and died, and found themselves walking in a new land. They talked to their parents and grandparents and others the white soldiers had killed. The new world was like the old world the white man had destroyed. There was peace, though long-dead people from other tribes also lived in this new land. All the Indian nations formed one tribe and could understand one another. Kicking Bear and Short Bull walked around and saw everything. Then the holy man of the Paiute brought them back to life again.

"You have seen the new land I'm bringing," he said. "The earth will roll up like a blanket with all the white man's fences and railroads and mines and telegraph poles."

Then the holy man taught them a new dance, a new song, a new prayer. He gave them sacred red paint. He even made the sun die; it was all covered with black and disappeared. Then he brought the sun back to life again.

This old uncle told me.

Then I saw it myself. People dancing, holding each other by the hand, singing, whirling around, looking at the sun. They had a little spruce tree in the middle of the dance circle. They wore shirts painted with the sun, moon, the stars, and magpies. They whirled around; they didn't stop dancing.

Some of the dancers fell down in a swoon, as if they were dead. The medicine men fanned them with cedar smoke and they came to life again. They told the people, "We were dead. We went to the moon and the morning star. We found our dead fathers and mothers and we talked to them." When they woke up, these people held in their hands rocks from the moon and stars. They clutched meat from the star and moon animals. The dance leader told them not to be afraid of white men who forbid them to dance this *wanagi-wachipi*. They told them the ghost shirts they wore would not let any white man's bullets through.

The earth never rolled up. The buffalo never came back, and the dead relatives never came to life again. Instead, it was the soldiers who came; why, nobody knew. The dance was not harming anyone, but I guess the whites thought it was a war dance.

Many people were afraid of what the soldiers would do. We had no guns any more, and hardly any horses. We depended on the white man for everything, yet the whites were afraid of us, just as we were afraid of them.

Then the news spread that Sitting Bull had been killed at Standing Rock for being with the ghost dancers. Some of the old people said, "Let's go to Pine Ridge and give ourselves up, because the soldiers won't shoot us if we do. Old Red Cloud will protect us. Also, they're handing out rations up there."

So my father and mother and uncle got the buggy and their horse and drove with us children toward Pine Ridge. It was cold and snowing. We were worried. Then the soldiers stopped us. They had big fur coats on, bear coats. They were warm and we were freezing. They told us to go no further, to stop and make camp. They told the same thing to everybody who came, by foot, or horse, or buggy. So there was a camp, but little to eat and little firewood, and the soldiers made a big ring around us and let nobody leave.

Then suddenly there was a strange noise, as if the biggest blanket in the world was tearing. As soon as we heard it, my uncle burst into tears. My mother started to keen as for the dead, and people were running around, weeping, acting crazy.

I asked my uncle why everyone was crying.

He said, "They are killing them; they are killing our people over there!"

My father said, "That noise—that's not the ordinary soldier guns. These are the big wagon guns which tear people to bits—into little pieces!" I could not understand it, but everyone was weeping, and I wept too. Then a day later—or was it two? No, I think it was the next day, we passed by there. My uncle said, "You children might as well see it; look and remember."

There were dead people all over, mostly women and children, in a ravine near a stream called Chankpe-opi, Wounded Knee Creek. The people were frozen, lying there in all kinds of postures, their motion frozen too. The soldiers, who were stacking up bodies like firewood, did not like us passing by. They told us to leave.

So we went on toward Pine Ridge, but I had seen. I had seen a dead mother with a dead baby sucking at her breast. The little baby had on a tiny beaded cap with the design of an American flag.

THE MASSACRE AT WOUNDED KNEE

Then suddenly nobody knew what was happening,
except the soldiers were all shooting and the
wagon-guns going off right in among the people. . . .
I wished that I had died too, but I was not sorry
for the women and children. It was better for them
to be happy in the other world.

—*Black Elk Speaks*

December 29, 1890

The buffalo lived in a house so the soldiers could not find them but the soldiers knocked on the door where the buffalo lived and asked if they had seen buffalo. The soldiers said they were coming in because it was cold and they were hungry. The buffalo let them in at first the soldiers didn't know the buffalo were buffalo. The soldiers piled their buffalo robes in the corner and the buffalo seemed to the men dark spots in the house though the chairs they sat in were buffalo and the table was a buffalo its knotholes were its eyes and the large heads turned as planets in the sky.

WOUNDED KNEE CEMETERY

I.

There was silence in heaven about the space
of half an hour.

—Revelation 8:1

Wounded Knee, South Dakota

Chief Big Foot
Mr. High Hawk
Mr. Shading Bear
Long Bull
White American
Black Coyote
Ghost Horse
Living Bear
Afraid of Bear
Yellowrobe
Wounded Hand
Red Eagle
Pretty Hawk
Wm. Horn Cloud
Sherman Horn Cloud
Scatter Them
Red Fish
Swift Bird
He Crow
Little Water
Strong Fox
Spotted Thunder
Shoots the Bear
Picked Horses
Bear Cuts Body
Chase in Winter
Tooth Its Hole
Red Horn
He Eagle
No Ears

Wolf Skin Necklace
Lodge Skin Knopkin
Charge at Them
Bear
Bird Shakes
Big Skirt
Brown Turtle
Blue American
Pass Water in Horn
Scabbard Knife
Small Side Bear
Kills Seneca

II.

We had been like wolves that gathered because we were starving. The animal we gathered around was the Ghost Dance. We moved in a pack. We circled. We circled. We stumbled as we danced. As we moved beyond our endurance. Our limits.

They came like a blizzard without end. They brought their unrest. We felt it in the air. *Break their teeth—their hold on the land. Drive them back, O Maker. They have no fear but themselves.*

Some were saying they saw the ancestors starting to return. They were like strange birds in flight. But our ancestors were the falling stars. I saw them at night on the open prairie.

We howled like wolves. Our teeth were on fire. We fainted. All hope was gone. In the confusion—soldiers opened fire—we were mowed down. We swallowed darkness.

The Sioux Uprising

1862, Southwestern Minnesota

We were warriors. We would make our mark. Our way of life was gone. Our land was gone. Our game was taken. We could not hunt. We were supposed to become Christian farmers like white settlers. We were not paid for the land that was gone. The summer was hot and dry. Nothing would grow.

At first there were four of us. We were Dakota, Mdewakanton band. The trader refused to give us supplies while we waited for what the government owed us. "Let them eat grass," he said.

Sometimes the soldiers gave us liquor. Sometimes we drank it until we couldn't feel our anger anymore.

We rode by a white man's farm. "Are you brave?" one of us asked. We killed the white man who had the land. But his wife, some neighbors, and a boy—we killed them also because they were there.

"Do you know what will happen now?"

We ran.

Little Crow declared war. We planned to kill all the whites, even the white soldiers who rode in from Fort Ridgely and Wood Lake and Fort Sill.

We were on the warpath. We killed the trader and stuffed his mouth with grass. We shot clerks. We shot the doctor who would not treat our children who died from the white man's diseases. We shot whoever walked by.

We couldn't stop. We rode onto their farms. We kept killing after they were dead. Stabbing and stabbing.

Some of the whites fled, but others stayed. They farmed and went on as though we weren't there.

Little Crow and the others fled wherever they could. But it was a matter of time. We were captured. Henry Sibley held military trials in the field. They lasted no longer than what it took a bird to fly from its branch. We were to be hanged. Three hundred and ninety-two men were tried; 69 were let go, 16 sent to prison, 307 were to hang. At least they tried us. Some wanted to murder us without a trial. President Lincoln commuted all but 39.

MANKATO HANGING

December 26, 1862

Afterwards we could speak of it, when we were in our *haven of rest*, as the minister called it. He stood with us on the scaffolding and told us we would be *blessed*. I don't know what I remember. We were hated even in death. There was no pity from the crowd. *Die, you snake!* Then we were in the black prairies of space. We tumbled over stars as we had prairie grass. The comets hissed. Sometimes I come back to the land. I feel the rope still around my neck. I was one of the hanged. It was a cold morning. My legs trembled. I could hear our teeth rattle. They put a blindfold over our heads. The minister prayed. The ramp fell. What were we supposed to do? Give up? Disappear? They kept coming. We knew they wouldn't stop. We sat in council asking the Great Spirit to lift us from the earth, to bring back the old ones, the buffalo, to make the white man disappear. We are in our own part of space now. The buffalo are fat, *un-hee*, the wind is free.

AFTERMATH OF THE SIOUX UPRISING AT MANKATO

We were held in prison at Mankato that winter. The cells were cold. Some of us died. When we lived outside, we didn't feel the weather, but in prison, shut in a room, we shook all the time with cold. There was not enough to eat. The guards taunted us, but we knew they were afraid. The white missionaries came to talk to us. Some of us hated their God. Some of us found God that winter. What did that mean? We heard the message that the white man's God was a Holy Man who wanted us to join Him. But we couldn't because we were not Holy; we were not Spirit. What was not Spirit in us they called sin. It was willfulness. It was not considering their God significant. It was not seeing their Holy Man as Holy. Our sin would keep us away from their God. But He had sent his Son, Jesus Christ, the one called *Nails-in-His-Hands-and-Feet.* God had to kill sin, had to kill what was not Him. God clothed Jesus in our sin and let the white men kill Him. Jesus took the sin someplace else. Then Jesus came back alive without sin, and if we called His Name, we would be like Him, washed of our sin. We thought about where Jesus had taken the sin, but did not know. We thought about this as we ate our hard bread and watery soup.

The white men told it to us over and over. We could not believe. We could not understand. We did not want to believe in the white man's God. We saw the white men killing and killing. Just like their God. What had we done wrong but defend our land? What had we done wrong but fight the white man who killed our buffalo, our way of life?

We had begun to hear of the Ghost Dances out west. There was a man who said he was this Christ. We talked about this to ourselves.

We could not believe in our sin. We lived as we lived. We didn't know what we did wrong. But we would see they were right—once we were in Christ. I listened to their words. One night I felt a warm spot in my ears. I thought their words seemed true. I knew what they said. I felt Truth from their side. I asked Jesus to be my Savior. I was washed of my sin. It made sense until I tried to explain it to the others. They mocked me. I tried to make them understand. Jesus was dead, but came back alive, just as the Ghost Dancers saw in the visions. I was no longer dead, but alive with Him.

Others had been hanged, but I was set loose.

I listened to the chant of their holy song.

Who could believe what we heard?

He was despised and rejected. He was a man acquainted with grief (Isaiah 53:3). He was from a God who sent his people to tell us about him, who did a great wrong to us, yet they have brought their God who would save us from the people who brought him. He had them bring it to us—this Christianity. This bitterness.

In the spring, savages as well as Christian Indians were transported to Dakota Territory, removed from the missionaries and the new state of Minnesota as far away as they could send us.

We were set loose, but to what? Our land was now a reservation. We were severed from our way of life. We could live in the open under a cottonwood arbor?

Hiawatha Asylum for Insane Indians

1903–1933, Canton, South Dakota

All that is left is a graveyard inside a wooden fence. The caretaker's house across a field. A cow barn, sheep and swine sheds.

The main building of the asylum dismantled brick by brick.

Not many patients released but through death. Causes listed: tuberculosis, syphilis. Other Indians buried elsewhere.

At the opening in the wooden fence, 120 names on a plaque: *Names of Indians Buried in the Cemetery.*

Some of the names:

Yells at Night
Big Day
Ne-Bow-O-Sah
Ruth Chief-on-Top
Blue Sky
James Crow Lightning
Sits-In-It
Lowe War
Trucha
James Blackeye
Guy Crow Neck
Willie George
Joseph Bigname
Baby Caldwell
Red Crow
Silas Hawk
Cecile Comes At Night
Amos Deerr

Two Teth
Long Time Owl Woman
Edith Standingbear
Kay-Zhe-Ah-Bow
Kay-Ge-Gay-Aush-Eak
Louis McIntosh
Dasue
Maud Magpie
Nancy Chewie
Mary Buek
Enos-Pah
Baby Ruth Enos-Pah

Here I stopped copying names.

Yells at Night d. 11-21-08

The sun turned its back. It was dark all the time in the cell but for a thin strip of light at one end of the trapdoor. Sometimes I tried to pick it away. Sometimes I tried to catch it. There were things moving in the dark. I sat in the corner with them touching. I crouched in the corner because the air above me was bigger than I could stand. I saw small balls of light. They were fingernails of the spirits in the pit. I heard their hands lift the trapdoor. The stars fell in, rattling as they scratched the walls.

Big Day d. 7-3-05

I worked in the gardens and wasn't hungry anymore. I ate until they kept me from it.

Ne-Bow-O-Sah d. 12-18-14

I tried to sing but they stopped my song, so I sang with my thoughts. I was the spotted one who called the sun from its hiding place. Because of the spotted one the sun came. I turned into a bird with spotted wings. I flew into the night until a blanket was thrown over me, my wings wouldn't open, my claws grip, my beak tears. The spotted one lifted me. The animals held in their barn. The pigs in confinement. They sang their thoughts with their song.

Ruth Chief-on-Top d. 5-15-18

I worked in the laundry. I washed and mended sheets bitten or clawed. Maud and Nancy wanted to run. Where would they go? The snow covered fields like sheets torn by roads. What would they do? There was no world left outside the asylum. How would they leave? Just walk down the road unnoticed?

Blue Sky d. 6-20-14

They wrote our names hardly listening to what was said. One had a name so long they called him Bigname, but it meant something like *Now-the-people-have-seen-the-darkness-the-prophecies-said-they-would-see-they-danced-and-this-is-what-came.* I worked in the crops, listening to what the fields said.

James Crow Lightning d. 3-8-21

The lightning had the strings of a straightjacket. The wind was a storm. They came and got me for thundering. How could I sit without moving unless I was wrapped with lightning? My arms could not hold still. They bound me at night. What was the council of my grandfather? The sky was empty without him. The strings of the lightning laced. I was a tree tied into place by the roots of its lightning. I untied the lightning. I ran through the field. I plunged into the Sioux River. I climbed the ridge to the east. I unlocked the roof of the cow barn to fly like the thunder. The wind unroped me. It hurt to be tied by lightning. My legs pulsed until I howled. They would find my feet purple and dead.

Sits-In-It d. 1-26-21

I thought in circles like someone lost in snow. I would not tell them my name. I would not move. "Sits-In-It" they called my name.

Lowe War d. 12-24-09

There were clowns climbing his head. In the cell there were loud noises of the circus. I heard horse. Cow. Pig. Sheep. Animals from another land locked in the asylum of their cages. Animals forced to be what they were not. Doing what they did not want to do. Living with their hearts caged. I saw a train. Animals dead to themselves, their eyes glazed. The thunder yelling—then only silence.

Trucha

It was a place for the trouble causers. For those burning with rage.

James Blackeye d. 5-6-22

The inmates were brought to the asylum in the night. By train or road. The blizzards howled. The train howled.

There was a stirring of sound from the cells below. A baby cried. We were ordered to be quiet. To hold our noises, our cries and moanings. But in the asylum we could hear the ghosts, the spirits, the old ones, the dead ones, until we descend into death. The world was insane. They brought it with them. It was the disease we caught like smallpox. They recorded our deaths. I dug the graves. Children were born there. This hell they invented in God's name.

Guy Crow Neck d. 9-6-27

He stands in the cell with a light in his head. He shows me the holes in his feet and hands. He says he is Light. He calls my new name. He speaks me into being. I have been said.

Auntie Opey

1938

Auntie Opey George wanted as far away from South Dakota as she could get. She had a relative (Willie George) who died in the Hiawatha Asylum for Insane Indians. She had a long and troubled history. She had dreams that were more than dreams. They were real, Auntie Opey said. She dreamed she was standing on the open prairie. On one side, there was land and air; on the other side, the land was gone. She was standing in a landscape, she said again. To her left, there was land and air; to her right, there was only air. Take one step to her right, and she'd fall into open space. She had a cat who was dead, yet she said in the mornings just before she woke, she could feel the cat beside her, curled in a ball the way she did when she was alive.

Auntie Opey George was raped by a rancher. She told her father, but he wouldn't listen. She ran away and married Earl Ruff, a man she met in a feed store, because her father wouldn't believe her. Afterwards, her father killed himself, first telling his brother, Lukus, to punish her for running away. Lukus (who in some accounts was her former husband) killed Earl, brought Auntie Opey back, imprisoned and tormented her (or his wife, Deercee, did, out of jealousy). After escaping from Uncle Lukus, Auntie Opey had twins, Anderson and Zekus, whom she left for someone else to raise because she ran away again. Much later, she escaped wherever she had been, and joined her sons. They recognized her, even after such a long time, killed Lukus, and bound Deercee to the back of a buffalo. For this, the spirits on the reservation visited Auntie Opey with madness, which caused her to wander restlessly all over South Dakota until she met Ralph Fustus and married him in Pierre, and when they died, they both were buried in one grave.

Sometimes there's several versions of the story, but it's the same story:

To be raped was to know anything could happen. I could say no. I could fight. But I would be raped. I knew I shouldn't go. I felt it. Don't go. But he aroused my curiosity. It was the attention I got from him. He wanted me. What was so fearful? Because he wanted me, to unwrap me. To break into me. Afterwards, I knew the body of a man on me. I knew his weight. The hurt of it. I would never be safe. It was a choice I made. To be raped at the boarding school. I was not innocent. I was easy.

There were hornets in the attic. I heard them buzz. I saw them enter and leave through an opening in the eave. I knew they were there. I wasn't afraid. I went to the attic to find them. I was outside the camp. I was outside both camps. His and mine. I should have been wrapped in a shawl, dancing at the powwow. I should have been dancing to know who I was. But that was taken from me. It was denied.

I ran away from school after the rape. There was a man in Centerville I married. I got a job in the drugstore and he came in. I slept in the back room. He knew I was there.

"What's your name?" he said.

"Opey George."

"You can come and take care of my children."

They called me Auntie Opey.

After I married him, my father killed himself with alcohol, antifreeze, and horse liniment from the dumpster, leaving a note telling his brother, Lucas, to avenge his death on me.

I had plans for you, my father said. You were to earn wages, send money.

Uncle Lucas found me. Took me back home. He tormented me and kept me in the barn.

Long afterwards, I escaped.

After I ran away, I gave birth to twins who were brought up by a farmer.

When they were grown, my boys killed my Uncle Lucas and tied his wife to the back of a buffalo.

Then I went mad.

My father's uncle Willie George died in the Hiawatha Asylum for Insane Indians.

I heard his voice.

You know the borderland between the real and unreal. Between what happens and what is imagined. There is a spirit world that moves with us. Moves above us. Or we move with it. Or it moves us. Uncle Willie George talked about the spirits he saw. The world divided between the darkness and the light. He was afraid of the nails the dark spirits flew into him. They infested our lives. But the dark spirits had more than us to worry about. They were at war with the spirits of light. In his bed, he heard the roar of the war planes. We received the fallout of their power. It was over us they fought. It was between themselves they fought more.

It is something that is still happening. It hasn't finished yet.

Great-uncle Willie George wasn't crazy. Just trouble. The authorities arrested him. He ended up at Hiawatha because they couldn't handle him.

I was cured and wanted as far away as I could get. I ran with my dance partner, the train, to Tithorea, the next town to the west.

In Tithorea, I married Phocus.

Both of us were buried in one grave.

Sometimes you find your story in history:

1) Antiope was raped by Zeus.
2) She ran away from her father and married Epopeus, king of Sicyon.
3) Her father killed himself, first telling his brother, Lycus, to punish Antiope. Lycus (who in some accounts was her former husband) killed Epopeus, brought Antiope back, imprisoned and tormented her (or his wife Dirce did, out of jealousy).
4) After escaping from prison, she bore twins, Amphion and Zethus, who were brought up by herdsmen.
5) Long after, she escaped and joined her sons; they recognized her, killed Lycus, and bound Dirce to the horns of a wild bull.
6) For this, Dionysus, to whose worship Dirce had been devoted, visited Antiope with madness, which caused her to wander restlessly all over Greece until she was cured.
7) She married Phocus of Tithorea on Mt. Parnassus, where both were buried in one grave.

A Time to Get in Gear

Shall the axe boast itself against the man
who uses it?
Is the saw greater than the man who saws?
Can a *rifle* strike itself against the man
who lifts it up?
—Isaiah 10:15

Hi'hi'hai'-yai!
Hi'hi'hai'-yai!

1982

A powwow van. Lodge poles tied on top. Teepee-hide folded underneath. The Two Teth family. Oh boy. Father Spud. Mammam. Girl-boy. Buzz. Heading east on I-94 to powwow in South Dakota. Traffic. Three spirits along the road. Father Spud stop.

The spirits get in. *Huh. Huh. Huh. Uh-uh.*

They go spudding down the road. Feathers hanging from the rearview mirror.

"What's up?"

"Got a man whose dog killed his son. The man went on a rage and killed the dog, a daughter, and his mother. We're going to call him back from the crazy world."

The spirits fight over who rides in front. Father Spud has to separate them. Puts two in back with Buzz between them; one in the third seat with Girl-boy. Father tells them he will stop the van and put them out on the road if they don't straighten up. They could forget their mission, let the man stay crazy. They are messengers from the spirit world. How could they fight? They should remember their mission from the Old One the way He intended.

The spirits look out the windows. They see the hawks in the air that like the currents above the highway.

"Where this crazy man?"

"We'll know the road when we come to it."

Father looks at Mammam. Another one of those.

Sometimes the sky is behind a blackout curtain, old and worn, and only sometimes can they see the light behind it. That is the stars at night. Other times the sun is all light and they wait for the blackout curtain.

"Why'd you hitchhike?" Buzz asks them. "Can't you get around on your own?"

"I thought you could get to the place you supposed to go," Mammam says.

"Nobody pick you up?" Girl-boy chuckles.

"Not many see us," the spirits say, talking at the same time until their voices sound like bees in the van.

Father Spud stops for gas. The spirits look at the ice machine. The convenience store.

The spirits have come with a message. That's what the spirits are. Messengers from the Messenger Himself. The High Plains Holy Drifter. He roams the world. His eye goes over the whole earth seeking who will recognize Him. Seeking who will take their eyes off the earth just once to see inside the sky. Or who will look hard enough they see the lessons just out of sight.

What's up is a puzzle. A game with the spirits. But what the Two Teths pick up is not a game—the Two Teths being Father Spud, Mammam, Girl-boy, and Buzz. What they pick up is a narrowing of the highway. Road construction. The highway lanes changing, the arrows showing the shift in lanes. The powwow van jagging on the highway, over the hump of road that crosses the median. Now the cars are single file in a lane on the other side of the highway. The oncoming ones from the other way don't like it either. Both lanes on their side are supposed to be theirs. Their cars frown as they pass. The road is theirs now. The Two Teths are the defeated and have to ask permission to pass on their side.

"Once two women claimed the same man as their husband." The spirits tell a story to pass the time. "They kept fighting until the messenger said, *Let's divide him, so each woman will have a half*, and the women agreed."

Mammam squirms in her seat. But not as much as Father Spud.

Sometimes something reminds the spirits of the old world, the world that was here before this one. Maybe the cutout of the Badlands they pass. Or a particular edge of the sky. Father Spud isn't sure. Then the spirits grow quiet. Or they ask to stop, but Father Spud keeps driving. He sees their longing for what they knew. He thought it would be over when he left the earth, and he would never look back.

The spirits bump against Buzz, who asks them to stay by the windows.

I come from the Father
I come from him.
The crow.
The crow.
I cry like it.
I cry like it.
Caw, I say.
Caw!

The spirits are cawing in the powwow van. What else can spirits do?

They don't caw too good.

"*Huh. Huh.* Uh . . . " one of them interrupts, "that was the road there."

"No—" the second one says.

"We're not there yet," the third one says.

"That the road we passed down to Pine Ridge?"

"Yop," Father Spud says. "South through a wedge of the Badlands. Then the prairie. Highway 44 to 35. Manderson to Wounded Knee to Pine Ridge."

"Turn around."

"There's another road ahead that goes to the same place," says Father Spud.

"That one's gravel," Mammam reminds him.

They turn around and take the road south from the interstate and drive through the dirt bluffs of the Badlands. Then the pastures with spotted horses. Mile after mile of prairie grass and a few hills. They drive past the white frame churches standing on the prairie. Little square boxes, cardboard-like, with a steeple.

The devil—*Hi'hi'hai'-yai!*
The devil—*Hi'hi'hai'-yai!*
We have put him aside—*Hi'hi'hai'-yai!*
The White Man Above.
He is our Father.
He is.

Them spirits—ha! They always making jokes.

When they are nearly to Pine Ridge, Father Spud turns onto a dirt road at the insistence of the spirits. *Howard Chewie* written on a mailbox crooked on its post. A dirt road to a rusted trailer, several sheds, broken-down cars. Too late to back out.

The man had a dog that mauled to death his only son. In his rage, the man got his shotgun, killed the dog, a daughter, and the grandmother, and wounded another daughter.

The rifle took over. He couldn't stop shooting. The rifle kept loading itself. Chewie's wife, mother, daughters tried to stop him. He shot at them, missing his wife and two daughters. He shot the trailer. He went wild. His eyes had snow in them, they said.

His mother had told him to watch the dog. Yet Howard Chewie neglected the danger. Ignored it, rather. The dog growled at the boy. The dog was not in the mood to tolerate children. Maybe it had been abused before it wandered onto the Chewie place. Maybe the boy reached down to him, maybe the dog thought the boy meant it harm, but the dog turned with a vicious bite to the boy's face, and once the injury was made, the blood, the screaming, something primal was loose, and the dog continued its attack until the child was dead. The dog lay in a bloody pool at the edge of the yard. The coroner's van had left with the bodies of the boy, the girl, the grandmother. The rescue unit had the other girl nearly to the hospital in Pine Ridge—a clinic, actually. What the spirits and the Two Teths found was a woman, Mrs. Chewie, Howard's wife, still crying, broken between sobs, and the two girls huddled together under the porch of the trailer where they often played. Howard Chewie had disappeared down the dirt road. Someone had come for the dog, or what was left of it, and carried off its remains.

The spirits talk to the girls under the porch. They ask Girl-boy to sit with them. They talk to the mother and ask Mammam to sit with her. They hear the police sirens. The police dogs. They want to find Howard Chewie before the police and the dogs do.

The spirits are standing in the yard and then they are gone. They move across the prairie without moving.

"Why didn't they do that to get here?" Buzz asks.

The police close in on Howard Chewie. He won't give up. They shoot. Howard Chewie is wounded. He falls. The dogs rush him. The police pull the dogs off Howard. They handcuff him. They pull him to his feet. He struggles. They hit him with their fists. He is in the back seat of the police car, stunned and cuffed. He is in a sleepwalk. The spirits get in the police car. The police don't know they are there.

The spirits sing their healing song.

We give him a name:
He could not stop shooting the gun.
He could not stop shooting the gun.
We take his finger from the trigger.
We take his hand from the gun.
We call him back.
We give him another name:
He will stop shooting the gun.
Now he will stop shooting.

Howard Chewie is in the hospital, under guard.

What is a shotgun to strike out on its own? The spirits talk to Howard Chewie. Should one of them stay with him? They argue. No one wants to stay.

The girl's in the hospital too, in another ward. The spirits take a lightbulb from their medicine bundle. From their parfleche they take a cord. They plug it in her room and light the blue lightbulb.

We touch the blue wound.
We touch the blue wound.
It is in her where she can't see.
It is inside her there.
We light the blue wound with blue light.
The light draws the hurt into itself.
We unplug it from the socket in the wall.
The blue wound is gone.
The blue wound is gone.

The spirits love electricity. They use it in their ceremonies whenever they can.

"Your father was going to shoot himself," the spirits tell her. "You stopped him before he did."

Now the Two Teths arrive at the hospital, which is more of a clinic, with Mrs. Chewie and the two girls.

"I want to go to the trailer," the wounded girl says.

"He shot it full of holes," Mrs. Chewie says. "You're better off here."

"We'll patch it for you," Father Spud says. Mamman, Girl-boy, Buzz look at him.

The spirits return to Chewie's place. They ask Father Spud to drive them in the powwow van, feathers hanging from the rearview mirror. Lodge poles tied on top. Teepee-hide folded underneath. The Two Teths could unwrap it in the Chewies' backyard. They could feed the tethered horse. Dig post holes for a fence. Help the girls through their nightmares.

The spirits have a healing ceremony with sage on the Chewie place. They have a cleansing ceremony in the trailer with sage. The brillo pad of the spirits. Comet scouring.

Holy. Holy. The Messenger Himself. The Maker. The Old One. Even the Two Teths hear voices in the sage. The spirits buzz the trailer. They think it has wings.

The Two Teths were on their way to the powwow. They were stopped. The spirits always intrude. Interrupt. They don't know a good powwow when they see one.

"That girl in the hospital is going to recover," the spirits tell Father Spud. "That's the powwow where we go."

In the two girls' nightmares, a family drives up. They unload their gear. Just what the Chewies need.

"Who are those people?" the girls ask.

"Their name is Two Teth," the spirits say.

"Two Teth?" they ask. "What's that?"

"The original name must have been Two Teeth. Who knows? What is One Teth? What is Two Teth? You go with what you got."

It is a thought they toss like a ball.

The Two Teths also try to sleep. Mammam paints the white sky black with a brush that spreads the paint thin. That's the night sky. The old white paint showing through as stars. Maybe the blackout curtain will cover them awhile. How could they fit in a world in which they don't belong? Not even to their own kind. Their own needy kind in trailers and tract housing.

"What do you want me to do?"

Mamman looks at Father Spud. "I'll know it when I see it."

"It's scary to dance at the powwow," Buzz is telling the two girls in the yard. "The drummers try to trick you. You think the drummers will stop but they go on. You think they will go on, but they stop. If you mess up, they don't let you forget."

"I think we got the van in reverse," Father Spud say. "Get it in gear. Let's move ahead."

The spirits sing their funeral song in the cemetery:

> They will eat pemmican—*E'yeye'yeye'!*
> They will eat pemmican—*E'yeye'yeye'!*
> We say so, we say so,
> The Father says so, the Father says so.

"Your sister's on a far road. She caught up with your brother," the spirits tell Mrs. Chewie and the girls. "Your grandma and that old dog trottin' there too." At that, Mrs. Chewie cries. Mammam tries to quiet her. She frowns at the spirit—the one doing all the talking. "We washed them with the ceremony," the spirits tell the Chewies. "They won't carry blood into the next world."

The son, daughter, and Howard's mother are in the afterlife. The spirits assure the wife, the two daughters who hover near their mother until it looks like their feet aren't touching the ground.

The dirt cemetery is pitiful. Twists of tobacco. Braided sweet grass. Medicine bundles with wads of sage. Hand-made crosses. A few stones. The prairie wind sweeps over them, nearly pushing them over. It isn't easy to stand on the prairie. One spirit loses his cap. Well, it was the cap he borrowed from Buzz. Buzz frowns.

Death. Death. They know it on the reservation. The reservation roads staked with white crosses. Accidents, alcohol-related. Driving is a form of suicide on the reservation. A wish to step into the sky. A release from hopelessness.

Mammam divides Father Spud with her words. Her complaints. Why are they still together? Buzz and Girl-boy reel from their fights. The Two Teths catch the Chewies' ball, and in that ball is their own strife. The red dog death. They are bit. They know the rifle. The rage. They step over that line. They are going to the same place. Disaster from which they never recover, despite the blue lightbulb of the spirits. No matter, the Old One Himself can patch them up. They have been hit. They have been defeated. They have been blasted with poverty. Alcoholism. Unfaithfulness to husbands. Wives. Beat kids. Get them shut up. Put the meanness in them. The mean red dog bite. They over there now. In the other world. The ancestors. The Chewies' boy and girl and grandmother and dog. They are beyond the peepholes of light. The peephole show of this life.

The Pine Ridge Gospel Church preacher preaches at the funeral. Christ. Christ.

Euchala.

Euchala.

Wadu.

"Which way is it?" Buzz and Girl-boy ask. "Is it this way or is it that?"

Father Spud goes to the Pine Ridge Hardware for rifle-bullet repair. The Two Teths plug the holes in the trailer. Buy window glass. But wrong size. Go back. How much trouble to put up fence? Trouble. They buy a bag of cement to set the posts in the holes. Girl-boy fixes the broken swing in the yard.

Are these spirits really here? Or are they a vision they encounter? A trick? A step into the other world? It is high summer. Yet the Two Teths see spirits with eyes like a whiteout blizzard.

The wounded girl comes back to the trailer from the hospital.

Howard Chewie is in jail for murder of his mother and daughter. Attempted murder of his wife and three other daughters. The trial upcoming. It will be quick. Guilty. Guilty. Every one of them.

Little Ghosts Running from Children

Some of our stories are absolutely ugly.
Those are the ones we need to tell.
—Gerard Baker, Hidatsa-Mandan

1959

We were brutalized and the terror was all ours. The nun tried to make it beautiful. She read us the lives of saints how they were beaten how they were sawed in half (Hebrews 11:36–37).

She never asked what caused our welts and bruises. She sat before us in school. Above her the Savior nailed to the cross. She must have thought of us receiving our blows. Our stripes like Christ's.

At night in our house we crawled into our bed pulled up our feet wore our shoes shivered until our breath ran like small ghosts.

In the mornings dull from drink our father knocked over empty bottles on the nightstand stumbled into the room. We shook with fear. We read his every breath when they deepened with anger. He marked our territory, made our sweat stink. We had nowhere to go.

The winter beat us with storms the summer with heat. A tornado wiped a few houses away. We listened to one another yelping crying out in pain our bodies jerking he beat us one at a time in front of one another or taking us in the other room what we heard worse than what we saw.

We walked to school teased a dog chained in his yard pelting him with stones until his fury jerked his body the chain so short he choked himself when he leapt at us flapped to the ground wild dog stupid with rage could not get us no matter what he did we pelted him until he passed out we thought he was dead but his spasms sucked breath into his body we left him there was nothing of himself he could hold onto.

Where did he learn to hit? What school he go to? The welt school. The whip school. The belt pound and hammer school. We laughed thinking of him learning how to beat we howled when he passed out before he beat us. We were wild with beauty.

Here he come with stick.

Who will get?

Who what done?

He watching?

What he see?

His stick fire.

Me he beat.

By his stripes we are healed.

We groaned in sleep we cried our dreams we peed our fear. The knowing it was ahead. But God didn't stop the death of his son, she said.

The dog there barken.

We barken back.

Louder he.

Louder we.

Shud up owner yell.

She showed us pictures of heaven and hell. Hell was most of it. Christ sat on his chair with a hole in the floor where he sent the unbelievers to be tortured. Dark as a prairie night with fire when a trailer burned. She said there was torture we could not imagine we would grow hollow our eyes would dry up. We would know terror that would take our breath. We would be staked to the ground. It would be hotter than summer and there would be nothing to drink for ever and ever. We would be alone though we were crowded together. There would be no light that was the worst part. There would be only voices wailing. Nothing we could see. We would feel snakes pass over us. They would enter our mouths. We would feel them moving through us. They would crawl in our bones. They would coil around our elbows and knees. Over us was the galaxy of light we could not see but knew was there and would receive reports of the rejoicing in heaven of which we never would be part. But we would know it was there and could have been a part if we had looked to Jesus who was busy sending everyone else to hell.

Are people whipped in hell? we asked but she didn't answer.

It was Growl face.

Dog rattle.

Snap tooth.

Snout face.

Jaw rattle.

Snap dragon.

Fizzle spit.

Wedge jaw.

Whip thistle.

Dog biscuit.

Roof roof.

Rib bones.

Show down.

She prayed for us to have vision of Christ but we saw the bad spirits over our father beating him with bark branches. Tying him into knots. We knew the yard was full of spirits we could not see but knew were there. They stood watching and if we looked they stepped behind the shed. They stopped up our ears with dust, filled our lungs with mud from the slough, blew windstorms in our heads. They holy men prayed. They had rituals to keep the bad spirits from us. We were tied to them corralled like the animals. It was hard getting through the world. Disease. Accident. The pressure alcohol lifts. Some of us kept leaving. Others of us made it. The bad spirits were hunters. One move and they knew where you were. You can't imagine how you longed for water. Or you talked to someone and they don't hear.

It was Musket face.

Yap yap.

Show gum.

Growl growl.

Scrap face.

Speech impediment.

Whoofa whoofa.

Snarl.

Sod buster.

Dust eater.

Wheeze wheeze.

Our father going nowhere. He roars at the spirits he sees. Our house where the bad spirits practice hell. He think he running from Wounded Knee? He think we cavalry?

Kicken up dirt with hind feet.

Revven engine.

Bark face.

Stiff back.

Fur rise.

Ridge back.

Zip dog.

Hizz hizz.

His self twist.

Remember when he was dog.

When my father stumbles on the ground he cries. We tell him Christ goes anywhere even to the bottom of our lives.

A Green Rag-Braided Rug

I.

In Memory of Richard S. Cardinal, Chipewyan,
1967–1984

The following document was found after Cardinal nailed a board between two trees and hanged himself.

I was born in Ft. Chipewyan that much I knew for certain, because it's on my birth certificate.

I have no memories or certain knowledge of what transpired over the next few years. I was once told by a Social Worker that my parents were alcoholic's and that all us kids were removed for this reason. I was separated from the rest of my family and placed in a foster home some-were in fort MacMurry.

My earlyiest memories are from when I was liveing with a family in Wandering-River. I have little memory of the home but I do remember that I was playing with some wooden matches and I guess when I left one was still going and the outcome was desastrous, the shed in which I had been playing had caught on fire, which spread and caught onto the hay stack. When they finally put the fire out and managed to save 3/4 of the stack I was given the wipping of my life . . . I was also reunited with my brother at this home so I did not feel so alone any more. We were moved after about a year.

Our next home was in the same town just a few miles away. This home was good in one way but bad in alot of ways. It seemed that for every good happening there were two bad ones . . . about three months later my sister Linda (who is the oldest of the girls in our family) was moved into our foster home. Charlie and linda were always playing together and seeing as I was still pretty small I was always left-out so I began to spend alot of time alone.

Our next move was a few month's later, we were moved to live ______________ where we lived with a elderly couple by the name of ______________. I enjoyed this home for the first two days then everything went wrong when we had to go back to school. The first day I was sent to the office three time's in the same day for fighting. . . . I began to get into a lot of trouble for neglecting my chores and was hit several time's with a stick and sent to bed . . .

[This next year] I was not considered an outcast . . . and got my first tast of puppy love with a girl named Heather. I was halfway through the school-year when a Social Worker came to our home and I was to be moved and asked me how soon I would be ready to move and I answered, 1 week, I should have answered never. When I would move alone Charlie and linda would stay.

I had 4 hours before I would leave my family and friends behind and since linda and charlie were at school, I went into the bedroom and dug out my old harmonica and went down to the barn yard and sat on fence and began to play to the cows. I didn't know how to play at all but I played real slow and sad like for the occation, but before halfway through the song my lower lip began to quiver and I knew I was going to cry and I was glad so I didn't even try to stop myself. I guess that __________________ heard me and must have come down to comfort me, when she put her arm around me I pulled away and ran up the road aways. I did'nt want no one's love any more I had been hurt to many times so I began to learn the art of blocking out all emotions and I shut out the rest of the world and the door would open to no one.

The Social Worker arived to take me away to my new home. On the way their he tryed to talk to me but I was'nt hearing or trying to hear. When we arrived the Social Worker wanted to talk to the parents alone so I remained in the car . . . I was taken into their house and ___________ showed me were I would sleep. The room was in the basement of the house. When I walked into the room I could not believe my eye's. The floor was covered with water and there were boards on the floor to keep your feet from getting wet. The walls had been painted red but had long before began to peel off, the window which was no bigger than a atlas had a gape between the foundation at the bottom which let in the cold winter wind and the beds were no wider than two feet across and about a foot off the floor. there was a 40 watt light that was in the ceiling and you had to pull a string to turn it on . . .

In the morning I was assigned chores to do and I would be fed after they were done. When I was finished I was returning to the house to eat and found a lunch bag in the door way, this was my breakfast. I was not allowed to eat with the family in the house, and the same with lunch and supper. The next few days were like living in jail, I was set boundaries in which to stay in and I was to come running when I was called. I kept telling myself that this was all a bad dream and I would wake up soon with charlie and linda and the rest of the family in our home back in Ft. Chipewyan, but in reality I knew that I would'nt wake up and that this was real, and not just some bad dream.

The first month's rolled by slowly and then bang! it was my birthday, I was nine however it seemed that everybody could careless. I remaind locked in my own little world and would and would not let anything in or out I was enrolled into Westlock Elementy School, I was better hear I was away from the farm and the family that lived their.

Here I began to fall into bad company and got into alot of trouble. We were let out of school two weeks for Christmas holadays. I figure things would eased-up abit between The Family and I during this period however I was wrong Things got worse. I was beginning to feel rejected and unwanted. Christmas morning I was sent outside and not allowed back in till dinner and even then I had to eat in the basement, This was it I couldn't take anymore of this I had to leave, go somewere were nobody would find me. I pack my belongings into my back-pack and I had stoled a bottle or rye so I packed that to the garage and rolled up the old tent and secured this onto my pack I was almost ready.

I went back into the house and got a box of wooden matches and stuffed it into my pocket's as I was comeing back-up the stairs and noticed for the first time the guns hung on the wall ther was a box below the gun rack and I opened It up. Beautiful I told myself, the box had pagages of shells for the guns. Each pack contained 3 boxes of fifty shells. I took two packs and stuffed them into my jacket. When I had got the gun out of the house to the garage. I slipped on my pack picked up the gun and head away from the house. I had been gone 4 days before I was caught and brought back to the farm however I felt as though I had done darned good since I was only 9 years old.

I spent the rest of the winter here feeling lonely and very depressed. And I began to think seriously about suicide. The first time I attempted it I used a rasor blade to cut my arms but it hurt so much I didn't try it again. When school started up once more I began to skip classes and the ____________ were informed. When I returned to the farm that evening ____________ was waiting for me and he began to yell and scream at me. I was'nt listening and did not care. finaly he blew his stack and hit me. It was the first time I was hit by him and I guess he exspeted me to start in bawling but I didn't I just stood there and stared blankly at him. This must have scared him because he backhanded me. My lip begin to bleed quite badly. When I tasted the blood I spit it beside his shoe's and told him to GO TO HELL, and with that I walked away while I left him standing there looking rather stupid.

After school I would do my chores and sit in the barn and think and one day I was in there thinking, and it struck me I could kill myself now and no one would know until it was too late, and it just so happenes that the bail I was sitting on had a bailer twine on it so I slipped it off and climbed up to the rafters. After I had secured the rope I climbed down and placed some straw underneath the rope I climed on and stood up determined to go through with it. I said a short Prayer for god to take care of my family. I placed the rope around my neck and kicked my lungs felt like they were melting right out of my head. Finaly I blacked out and was engulfed in a blanket of black.

Unfortunately I woke up. I could see alot of people above me, all of a sudden thay all began to talk to me at the same time. I could not make out what they were saying all the words were echoing in my head and my eye's would not focus in on the people above me then I was swept back into a sea of blackness.

I was released from the hospital after about a week. I was returned to the ____________ family my social worker was there. We sat and talked for about two hours about how things were going. I exsplained to him that I wanted to return to ____________ and I wanted to be with Charlie and Linda, however he tried to exsplaine to me how that was impossible for me to go back because . . . she was getting too old for so many young kids to take care of an eventually the ____________ would get another boy my age . . .

II.

I was born in Ft. Chipewyan that much I knew for certain, because it's on my birth certificate.

I have no memories or certain knowledge of what transpired over the next few years. I was once told by a Social Worker that my parents were alcoholic's and that all us kids were removed for this reason. I was separated from the rest of my family and placed in a foster home some-were in fort MacMurry.

My earlyiest memories are from when I was living with a family in Wandering-River. I have little memory of the home but I do remember that I was playing with some wooden matches and I guess when I left one was still going and the outcome was desastrous, the shed in which I had been playing had caught on fire, which spread and caught onto the hay stack. When they finally put the fire out and managed to save 3/4 of the stack I was given the wipping of my life . . . I was also reunited with my brother at this home so I did not feel so alone any more. We were moved after about a year.

Our next home was in the same town just a few miles away. This home was good in one way but bad in alot of ways. The new foster parents were strict and I had to go to church. It seemed that for every good happening there were two bad ones . . . about three months later my sister Linda (who is the oldest of the girls in our family) was moved into our foster home. Charlie and linda were always playing together and seeing as I was still pretty small I was always left-out so I began to spend alot of time alone.

Then my foster parents brought another boy about my age into their home and I had someone to play with. They talked to Charlie and linda and told them that sometimes they had to play with us. We had stories at night and when I went to school the teacher told them I was behind and had to learn some at home too. They helped us with homework and told us stories of the Chipewyan and when I didn't do my chores one night I went to bed without dinner and after that I didn't neglect my chores. It was alot of work to have foster children and everyone had to work hard. When I got in trouble at school for fighting I had to stay after school and my foster parents didn't get me until dark. They told me I shouldn't waste my time fighting. They saw the stories I could write and they asked me to tell them at night and Charlie and linda and the others had to listen. On cold nights in the open room of the upstairs I sat on the round, green rag-braided rug and told a story. I had an iron bed that creaked when I got into it and a three-drawer wood chest with light green paint.

The next year I got my first tast of puppy love with a girl named Heather. Charlie and Linda knew I liked her and they teased me. I fought with Charlie and got a wipping but not as bad as when I started the fire in the other place. I still liked matches. I liked the spark and the small yellow tongue of flame. It was only air but air that had a story about it. It could lick other things and give them its flame. Sometimes I watched my foster parents light the wood stove with a kitchen match and some wadded-up paper and wood. I felt the warmth spread across the room. The fire was there—its heat, though the fire itself stayed in the wood stove. The match was a small stick but it could start a roar. But it was a roar that got out of hand pretty quick if it got loose. I had learned that and didn't want to repeat it.

I wanted to write a story about a match. A match explodes into fire when struck on the head. I had stolen matches in the first place I lived. I had struck fire that lit the haystack. A match was an oar on a river of fire. It brought down a stack of hay. When I struck matches I had something from another world. I had power. I had caused heat and light. I wanted the magic of blaze, of burning, of running fire. But I couldn't stop the fire. It ran away from me and I was sorry I struck the match that burned the hay. I was amazed it caught and spread but amazement turned to fear. Look what I had done. His words when he came after me were a flame.

It was my birthday and I sat at the table next to my foster father and got presents that was a new shirt and a tablet for writing my stories. Charlie said paper wasn't a present—he didn't want it anyway who would? But I wrote Heather on the first page and told how I gave her a cookie I saved from lunch and she thanked me.

And Charlie and Linda and George and me sneezed and coughed and were sick at Christmas—our foster parents gave us medicine and we got better and opened our presents. And Linda could light the kerosene lamp in our room and I watched the flame—the combustion of a yellow point of air that was only air but it was like a story that was only words but words that carried a small tongue of flame.

I thought the combustion of alcohol was like a flame—it was the fire my parents needed.

We were fighting and tumbling in the upstairs, the attic, of our foster parent's house—Charlie and Linda were teasing me and we were fighting and Charlie gave me a bloody lip and our foster parents came with a belt and corrected us and told us a story from their Bible and we had to sit and listen to it and be quiet and my lip was throbbing and the blood tasted like the iron post of my bed.

> And he [Elisha] went up to Bethel: and as he was going some children came out of the city and mocked him, saying, Go up, you bald head; go up, you bald head. And he turned back and looked on them and cursed them in the name of the Lord. And two bears came out of the woods and tore forty two of them. (II Kings 2: 23–24)

We looked at our foster parents who sat before us and didn't say anything for a while. We listened to the silence of the attic room and knew we would be out on the road by our own doing like those children, and who knew what bears would come from the woods.

III.

2004

It was education that got me out. And that barely. To gather voices to make the papers I wrote. To teach different points-of-view to say here we are. To finish a thesis on the Ghost Dance, which somehow caught my interest when I was at first drifting. To attend conferences invited to speak as one who was and will be. To be the first native to give a lecture at my own university on the native experience in the native voice.

I tell you, the Ghost Dance was not a frantic dance against annihilation. It was older than the white man. There always was the belief the dead would return, or we would return to them. Some came and said the dance was new. They came and turned it around. They never could get it straight. Those who wrote it down. The Ghost Dance was not a dance of despair. I tell you, it was based on a knowledge of loss and restoration. It looked Christian because of its similarities to their apocalyptic beliefs. Sometimes the same patterns develop on both sides of the fence. We only listened to the Christians because parts of their beliefs were similar to ours.

Because we did not have ammunition, education gave us the fire stick, the matches, the target. *Get them out of suicide. Outsmart death. They aren't going to the hereafter by their own hand.*

This is something like the westward movement across the country. Covered wagons and struggle. The land rough and travel hard that left people in its wake. The story has to be cut up. Only parts can be told at a time. Some of it left in silence. Some scrambled among others. Otherwise they would say this document is too depressing. It isn't true. Nonetheless, the job of stories is to remember. Memory keeps us here. That's why stories are important. I say first you have to listen to the story, and the story within the story. The ghosting of a story put here for remembrance. Sometimes I am a raging scholar.

My foster father lifted us above the ground level. The war zone. Where alcohol and drugs and despair took prisoners. Who were captives to it. Yet some made it. Maybe it was church that made the difference, but I'm not sure what happened there or why I don't always go.

What do you do in church? Some of us were there, for a while anyway, but cars wouldn't work, people couldn't find a ride, they'd been out late the night before and couldn't get up, they were sick, they were poor, they were discouraged.

Is it possible to go back and change history? Or at least keep it from happening again? Those dark and silent years when my parents let them take us away. Then the world pulled out our bones. Snuffed out life in us.

A story can never change the past. It can't bring anyone back. But it can be an after-trail saying the people longed for a place to belong. Their leftovers are still here.

IV.

Nuva' Ka Ro'rani'!
nuva' ka ro'rani'!

nuva' ka ro'rani'!
nuva' ka ro'rani'!
nuva' ka ro'rani'!
Gosi'pa' havi'ginu'!
Gosi'pa' havi'ginu'!

The snow lies there—*ro'rani'!*
The snow lies there—*ro'rani'!*
The snow lies there—*ro'rani'!*
The snow lies there—*ro'rani'!*
The Milky Way lies there,
The Milky Way lies there.

I worked with a Paiute song that seemed perishable, a bundle of twigs, going around and around, going nowhere with vocables—the *ro'rani'!*s, or extensions of language—sound actually making a place for further possibilities. Nothing happens without the voice, which is an energy field that speaks-into-being (nothing is that did not come from words). Native *song* means "breath" or "that-which-is-life" or "the-maker-of-life." The vocables, as I said, serve to cover anything not said that needed to be said.

But this song is not perishable, but provides necessary assurance. It is a song from the Ghost Dance, the late 1880–90 messianic dances that were thought at first to be a trail for the return of buffalo, ancestors, and family who died with the coming of the cavalry and the settlers. The song is for the voices caught in the path of the coming world. As it turns out, the Ghost Dance was not for the returning, but for the leaving.

Can you imagine Walt Whitman in the attic of his brother's house in Camden NJ closing his *Leaves of Grass*, and Emily Dickinson working in Amherst MA in solitude as the Paiute made their song of departure in western Nevada (*Nuva' Ka Ro'rani'!*)? They danced and chanted their words in the basin of the Sierras. The mountains were spotted with snow in the moonlight; the sky was spotted with stars. The repetition of words in the dark night and their hopeless situation brought trance and vision—the snow on the mountains was joined to the Milky Way, the path to the hereafter. In the song, the Paiute entered the universe. They were *roadward* (a vocable to extend "the-road-with-an-end" to "the-road-where-there-is-a-way").

I flew to South Dakota to talk with a man I had met at a conference. I wanted to talk further with him about my work on the Ghost Dance. It would become my doctorate. It would become my first book. I remember the round fields, the ones irrigated by water wheels, the first time I saw them from the air. They reminded me of the green rag-braided rug in the upstairs of our foster parents' house.

These are the notes that appeared as they were.

His great-great-grandfather had gone to those dances. He said they slept in tule lodges. In pine-bough arbors. He had told it to his son, who told it to his son, who told it to his. They ate fried bread, watermelon, rabbit stew, boiled coffee. His great-great-grandfather saw the blowings, the trances, the shaking. When he dreamed, he saw the other world.

On January 1, 1889, there was a total eclipse of the sun. The sun died and came to life; so will we, his great-great-grandfather had said.

The Ghost Dance arrived at the Mason Valley post office. They were sent to another place from there, the man said, adding his own comments.

They danced near Mount Grant. There was fire in the center of the earth. They knew it was there. The lake tried to rise up, extinguish the fire, but the sage hen kept it dry. ["The earth plays with matches"—I added my own comments.]

They flew above the earth as smoke from the sacred mountain. Above the smoke from the sage and cottonwood fires. I ask you what would you do? In brokenness we were formed. In brokenness we were framed. We thought we were whole, but we were wrong. We were in darkness and we could not stand on the ledge of change. We realized our weakness. What can I say? We were in anguish. The Maker thundered at the head of his army. It was a momentum. We were swept under. This we share because another momentum comes. Our old stories say. We don't know when. We are rubble before the Maker. It is his mystery. When we were pushed out of the world, there were provisions. There was a way.

But he said his father said his father said that his father said that Wovoka gouged his hands and feet with his own knife to look like the Christ. That Wovoka, that Paiute Jesus. Yes, he survived a fever. He survived death.

If he was not Jesus, he brought hope. He brought vision. Yes, but he made his own marks.

This trembling, this going away to the other world. A shuffle of the feet. The repetition of the chant. *The snow lies there. The snow lies there.*

They quaked and fell rigid and stiff as a tree.

They were dreamers. They saw into the other world. They went there and came back. They brought a dance back from the other world, close as a shadow and its cottonwood. In the dance, they passed between a cottonwood and its shadow. They were merchants from the other world.

There was a final day for them, yet the earth went on. It ended with Hotchkiss guns, howitzers, a cold, starving, desperate people, some of whom would survive to know suffering, hunger, annihilation of their way of life, and the hopelessness of their dreams. The Big Foot band had been called "hostiles." There were battalions of soldiers. Cavalry. Infantry. His great-great-grandfather heard it where he was. It was another day the sun died.

Imposters. All of us.

They closed that which was coming. Now the darkness that covers the land.

But in winter, the sagebrush is capped with snow like the Milky Way spread on the earth as a blanket so thin you could see the darkness through its light.

Wherever it was, his great-great-grandfather was close to it.

A new world will come, the buffalo, the elk, the old ones. All will return. Those who don't belong will have to leave.

Something, whatever it was, has not passed, but stayed in its dormant shape to dance again on the land.

They would not be lifted, but pass through the dark years before them.

Their disappointment, their anger. Their brief time to dance. To them it was everything. To them it was nothing. To them, it was somewhere in between.

The next month, I flew to Reno, Nevada, and rented a car and drove just over a hundred miles south through the desert to Walker Lake. Nothing was there. A camper in the distance, the ground smeared with pelican droppings, spider webs strung like miniature universes across small rocks. I drove into Schurz on the Walker River Reservation past a church and a cluster of houses. I saw a man sitting in his yard in a green metal chair and stopped to talk to him. Beyond us was Mount Grant in the Wassuk Range. Mr. Hanjar told me Walker Lake was evaporating because of upstream diversions. He told me his wife would fix us lunch. As we talked in the yard, I thought for a moment I could almost hear them—the Ghost Dancers. But then a car passed and the air was silent again.

As I drove back north, it seemed to me the Ghost Dance had been a struck match—a miniature volcano—a little flame of light.

Circus

He was caught into paradise, and heard unspeakable words, which it is not lawful for a man to utter.

—II Corinthians 12:3–4

1974

He would have joined the circus, but the circus was gone, across the Dakotas anyway. Maybe in other places there was still money to haul animals and equipment. He would have been a buffalo rider. A stunt man jumping through rings. But the circus had disappeared. Now there were carnivals with rides, games, concessions. A carnival was a counterfeit circus, but he joined when one came through Pierre. They traveled the highways in a convoy of old trucks coughing exhaust fumes over the land. Mobridge and Strausbury in South Dakota. Hurdsfield, Finley, and Halstad in North Dakota. Climax and Crookston in Minnesota. He would have hauled water for the circus animals. Buffalo. Horses. Coyotes. Clowns. Seeing how many they could get in the car after drinking. His mother had married again. He began to see that he didn't have a place there anymore. No man wanted a boy from another marriage, especially a boy growing bigger than he was. He was in the way. That was the thought that occurred to him on his way past old man Nagaset's place. Where could he go? What could he do? His father, Harold Blust, had been a minister. Harold had gone to boarding school and had liked the discipline, the regiment it had given his chaotic life. Later, he had started Pierre's Fundamental Holiness Mission. Then he was killed in a freak accident. Gerald's mother rolled through several marriages until he began to feel pushed out. What made his father see what others hadn't? Gerald had visions too. He had seen a wheel of cars twirl above him. There seemed to be a wheel of cars over that wheel. He was in one of the cars and it twirled until he was dizzy. He tried to call them to let him out, but no one was there. He didn't know how far off the ground he had traveled. Maybe it was a vision like the old ones had. The Ghost Dancers. He was a road man. A carnival man. He had untied his past. He wouldn't say much when anyone asked. He had loosed his hold on earth. He had played with suicide, driving blind at night with headlights off, with only the dim stars to light the road faster and faster until they became white crosses on the remote and distant roads. It was epidemic on the reservation—even in Pierre, where his father had moved. But he always had made it. He had not been able to kill himself.

He still wanted to play with pistols and bullets until darkness opened like an empty box. *Space shirt. Falling star-shirt printed with hands. Comet. Retro Rocket.* These were his names, more than Gerald Blust. In his vision, one car left the spinning circle of other cars and made a blurred passage through a blurred terrain, something seen at a distance, still out of focus. His ancestors had danced the Ghost Dance more than a hundred years ago; their steps were still on the earth, their yearnings and sufferings and seekings for the old ways to return, yet they would not return in this place, but were transferred to another—that other world where the Ghost Dancers had gone. Sometimes in the night he saw his own visions. He was booming. He passed stars dancing on the old grounds. Sometimes he passed trucks—not garish like the carnival trucks with their dents and chipped paint. How many of them had it taken to pack up the land, the arbors and circles where they had moved their feet until they fell into oblivion?

Holton Price, the carnival owner, asked Gerald to drive one of the carnival trucks when the carnival left a town late one night after the usual driver had been arrested for indecent exposure. Cyrus, the old man who had once driven that particular truck, the Ferris wheel truck, rode with him. His dog sat between them. Cyrus had a tendency to fall asleep. Holton Price soon discovered Gerald could drive, stay awake at night, unload the truck the next day at whatever town they'd arrived in. Cyrus was not a talker either, and they got along. Gerald tried to overlook the carnival and think of the circus he had seen in the movies. He thought of the circus as a Ghost Dance. The circles of dancing. The animal spirits over them. The ringmaster was the Holy One himself riding his white horse. The ancestors were acrobats on their high wire. As the carnival trucks moved relentlessly across the land, Gerald saw those visions at night. Once, even, the dog growled.

"Deer?" Cyrus asked, coming awake.

"Yes," Gerald answered, though his visions were not of this world.

Old pieces of his own life also came back as they traveled at night. It was the words he missed. Those words of memory were headlights into the darkness ahead.

Not all the bones had been there. Not the head, nor the feet. He could almost hear his friends.

Someone carried them off.

Or an animal.

An animal wouldn't carry off a skull and leave the smaller bones.

There were two girls murdered a long time ago. Well, the family didn't know they were murdered. They were missing. They didn't come home and were never seen again. Sometimes their grandmother said she could hear their voices in the wind. They were calling to her that something had happened. They had been afraid, but were not afraid anymore.

Old man Nagaset down the road had called them as they passed on their way to school. They made stories that it was him. But it was someone else. Sometimes they could hear old Nagaset rustling bushes, foraging around the place. He said he hadn't killed the girls—it was someone who had moved on. Old Nagaset didn't know any more than anyone else. But when they passed his house, they had walked with the girls between them, even girls they didn't like.

How could he tell them his visions of circling cars? They would laugh.

The Indians were the walls of Jericho that had come down.

At night, when they pulled into a town, it always looked hopeful under the blinking streetlights and the dim signs of convenience stores and Dairy Queens, but in the morning light, Gerald saw the poverty, the dullness. How easy it was to disappear. He thought of his mother. He called to let her know where he was, but his stepfather answered the phone. He said he'd pass the message on.

His father, Harold Blust, had preached that among the imposters, the quacks, there came a real one. He believed despite the jigging of the Ghost Dance, Jesus spoke to the Indians. No people went to the void without witness. He came to his people among the brambles and chaos. Among the hopelessness he was Hope. Despite the boarding schools, the immense and everlasting plague of the church in its unchristian behavior, among the savage brutality, the abuse, he was and shall be. Sometimes the church wore an unholy costume. That had been Harold Blust's conclusion. His wife's later husbands were a tilt-a-whirl away from Gerald's father, her first husband. How roped up she must have felt to fling so far after his death.

You know the Ghost Dance was a phenomenon among the Indians. They were backed to the ledge of the world and made to jump off—much like the games Gerald and his friends played as boys, jumping out of the only large tree on the north edge of Pierre, or off shed roofs. They were always playing with suicide. It came with being Indian with the dead-end road ahead of them. His people had been vanquished. It was not always true that traditions lived and hope was renewed. They had a ravaged history. They were in the way of those who came. It wasn't over yet. No one knew what was ahead for America. That two-edged country. The helper of the world. The destroyer. In the end, what was waiting for it? Generous nation. Despot. With a spattered history. A contradictory history. A conflicted history. A history not fully told. There was enough hurt and loss in them that they could crack like a branch heavy with ice. It was in the dreaded winters that hurt arose. His father had driven through blizzards setting houses back upright, calming children, keeping fathers from destroying themselves with drink that took them down. Winter was a lion they had to face without weapons. Why wasn't he like his father? Gerald had taken the first exit that came through Pierre—the carnival, with its calamities of broken-down engines and rides that leaked oil. Carnival workers were wolves with eyes toward their prey. Even Gerald felt their advances, but he slept with the carnival dogs that growled when someone came near.

The people in the small towns looked at him. The girls seemed drawn to him. Maybe it was his black hair. *An Indian*, he heard one parent say as he moved on, calling his two children to keep up, the children following reluctantly, looking back at him as they moved ahead with their father. He had followed his own father, but had not gone to boarding school. In Gerald's school, there were sniffings, inhalings, drinkings. They had their own language. They had despair. Sometimes at night in the boarding school, his father said he had listened to the crying. No one made fun of anyone then because they all knew the source of the grief. His father preached about their broken history. Almost every week, the sermon was about the bees in the carcass of the lion—Judges 14:5–14. Samson killed a lion on his way to Timnah. When he returned, a swarm of bees and their honey were in the carcass of the lion. *Can someone say "Hallelujah"?* his father had asked. He had two old ladies in his congregation. *Hallelujah*, the one said from the front pew. *Hallelujah*, the other answered from the back. Out of the carcass of the lion came the bees. One of the women's grandchildren stood on the pew with his arms outspread. The church shook. The motor revved. They flew over the land. Gerald named the carnival rides as he unloaded them: *Parable. Faith.* Holton Price laughed. Gerald heard the motor of the truck he drove, like a swarm of bees. The carcass of the Ghost Dance. Is that what he saw on the road late at night? Is that what led him through the darkness with the other trucks following? Was that the bee honey that was there for him? Was the carnival the bee ride that came from the carcass of the circus? Wasn't it true people in the Bible migrated from place to place like the carnival? Yes, once his mother remarried, he could have used a boarding school.

Gerald Blust drove now at the head of the convoy. Holton Price put him there. Cyrus was the map reader because he had been over the carnival's route for years. Sometimes Cyrus began to talk about his past. Sometimes Gerald talked of his. His story unfolded from the beginning. There were whole chapters of buffalo, horses, coyotes. Then the Ghost Dancers that had been massacred and buried in a trough at Wounded Knee. This was how it was. This was how his grandfathers ran from the Seventh Cavalry. It was now in the folds of the map: what used to be.

"Where you from, Cyrus?"

"Missouri. I left a family. Just up and moved out. The woman was nagging, had everyone calling me Billygoat Gruff. I got tired of her mouth. I wonder what happened to the children. Them I regret."

"Who was Billygoat Gruff?"

"I think he was a dwarf who lived under a bridge and wouldn't let people cross."

Now this was the way Billygoat Gruff told stories. They were walking up there by the brush and there was an old house fallen in on itself and they looked inside the hay and found bones.

Gerald told Cyrus about his father, Harold Blust, who had died in an accident. He was driving on a road and a cab light came loose from a passing truck, whirled through the air, into his open window, and hit him in the throat. Harold Blust may not have known what happened. The passing truck didn't know what happened either until the sheriff found the truck with a missing cab light.

The name of Gerald's mother's second husband was Billy Blue. The women were crazy about him. He traveled for the rodeo, of course. What else does a handsome man do who gets women to pay his entry fees, to buy him shirts and boots, saddles and bridles? *Shiftless*, his mother said, but that was her opinion. She didn't like the women he kept company with. The rodeo circuit, the traveling show. That's what he did. Travel from one woman to another.

The old voices came back in his father's house when the world was whole, before it was folded.

"I got a house I could return to in Pierre," Gerald told Cyrus. "It's a house my father left my mother, but she's living with another husband now. It has two rooms with an old leather couch and a bed with a blue-and-white checked spread. There's a photo of my father on the chest of drawers, another on the shelf. My first stepfather's rodeo memorabilia."

"I thought you said you didn't have much to do with your stepfather."

"I went on the circuit with him once."

It was the buffalo that took the girls. The buffalo that killed them. They smothered them with their weight. And scattered some of their bones. Maybe it was a man dressed in buffalo skin. Buffalo were grouchy. Billygoat Gruffs all of them.

From Crookston, Minnesota, they were nearing the North Dakota border about one in the morning. Holton Price radioed about stopping at a truck stop outside Grand Forks. Cyrus was nodding off by then. Gerald picked up the map. He thought they were almost to Carrington and said to go on. There were places the carnival couldn't stop.

Places they packed up and drove off in the middle of the night, maybe leaving one of the dogs behind by accident, hoping it would find them, following a thousand miles like those stories you hear, except the carnival didn't travel a straight path, but cut crosswise and crisscrossed the country, traveling back roads and staying off interstates and main highways. Staying clear of trouble. They followed old paths, stopping sometimes at new places. It was a circuit Holton Price set up years ago.

The carnival wasn't bad, if you didn't mind the lice, the rain, the heat, and sleeping on the ground. Even in a tent, it was still on the ground. No, Gerald changed his mind—the carnival was not an easy life. The carnival workers ate beans and stew cooked in an open pot. They slept under the trucks, or on the truck beds. They were dirty. They cheated one another. They loaded up. They moved on. Sometimes after driving all night, Gerald was afraid to sleep. Afraid he'd run off the road. He wasn't driving, he told himself; he had to sleep. Finally his body jerked and he slept in a fitful sleep until first light. Usually he dreamed of those hawks sitting in scattered trees beside the highway, watching the convoy pass. They just sat there looking. To Gerald, they were ghosts from the old dance.

From Grand Forks the convoy continued west on Highway 2. At Emerado, Gerald turned south on a dismal road toward Highway 200 where they would head west toward Carrington, North Dakota. Gerald noticed the gas gauge was low. Before long, the truck would begin to sputter. Maybe they should have stopped. The rest of the convoy must also be nearly out. Holton Price radioed for them to stop under the great wide night. Gerald looked at the map under the flashlight. There was a fold in the map from which he pulled out another hundred miles they hadn't counted on. Holton Price was in a rage.

"Get out," he ordered Gerald.

Gerald knew Holton Price had left sick carnival workers in clinics. Or in state hospitals for alcoholism or disease of one kind or another. Or for insubordination. One hundred miles were in the folds and the carnival nearly out of gas, out of steam. And he had to tell them they had another three hours.

Anyone in trouble got left behind. Anyone not at the carnival when they left was left behind. The carnival waited for no one. The carnival cared for no one.

"Get behind the wheel, Cyrus," he ordered. Holton Price had a soggy spirit. He was muddy inside. Gerald tracked away what he was. The convoy left Gerald on the black road. He looked at the sky above him. He thought of the land. The jackals. The wolves. The coyotes. Who knew what was there? He shivered in the cold without a jacket. Even summer nights had a chill. He walked along the road. It was so dark he could hardly tell what was ahead. There were chapters he didn't see. Whole generations still in the folds. When he spoke to the dark, the Ghost Dance danced in its unfolding. Gerald heard what he thought were buffalo, though he could also hear the convoy rattling ahead in the distance. Yes, probably there had been an old buffalo trail nearby. Maybe he could see their old wallows if it were daylight. Their voices were there. They had a story. Were the old disgruntled ones making a ring around him to keep him from harm? The only buffalo were now on ranches. Can you imagine buffalo crossing the interstate? They could put a stoplight there. There was a swale near his father's house in Pierre where settlers had crossed their land.

Now Gerald heard more voices than he knew. They were garbled like the old language, the holy language that carried stories he no longer knew, but knew were there. What did those crazy voices mean? He could not understand the old language, though he tried to remember his grandmother and grandfather and those speakers. Were they the ancestors? The wind in the leaves? Old Nagaset rustling bushes? Maybe Nagaset was one of those spirits that could travel at night longer distances than possible and return before light. Crazy old sheriff out there digging on the old place to see if there were other bones. Would the same thing happen to Gerald? Would his bones join the others? Would he become one of the stories of human bones? He had wanted to pass from the earth, but now that the possibility was there, he felt fear.

Old pieces of his life came back again.

There bear around here anymore?

I haven't seen one in years. Maybe farther in the hills.

You walking around the earth with your eyes closed.

I don't like what I see when I open them.

The convoy rode into the prairie as if it were a sea, as if the trucks were ships on the open sea, the rides with wings folded up inside like metal insects, or coiled like those worms that bored into ships. They had left Gerald behind to drown. Not one car passed on the remote road. Not one yard light shined in the distance. If he kept walking, would he come upon the carnival camped in a field until daylight, when some of the men would go ahead for cans of gasoline? Or would he be mauled by an animal? The carnival had a walk-through fun house of sorts. Sometimes Gerald worked inside, maneuvering one of those awful faces. Why was he following the carnival? There was nothing else. But it had put him out on the road by himself. His heart swelled and crowded his throat. Maybe he hadn't made it after all. The circus spirits still lived. They had been a reservation they carried city to city, town to town. Maybe Gerald would join them in the afterlife. How many discouraging times had his father, Harold Blust, stepped to his pulpit before a handful of people at the Fundamental Holiness Mission before he whirled off into the air? Gerald thought he still could hear his father preaching. It was their dark history they had to look into. Their shortcomings, their downfalls. Hadn't they looked enough? Was there still more to be seen? To be realized? More pain to be felt? To cover with alcohol? When they spoke to one another, the Ghost Dance danced. The long and devastating past began to heal. That was their new Ghost Dance. Whatever it took to reconcile. They told their stories. They made them heard. They said this is what happened to them. It killed them. It took what they were. Their land. Their way of life. Theirs was the loser's story. Look at it the way it was. A long and pitiful way of reclaiming tradition. Whatever it took. Gerald regretted that the pastor who replaced his father did not have his father's fire. He probably would lose the remaining members of the nearly nonexistent congregation at the Fundamental Holiness Mission.

You never knew what would happen, Gerald thought as he walked on the road in the dark. Once he was playing with his friends and uncovered some bones that turned out to be human. There were a lot of strange happenings—his father hit in the throat by a flying light. Fitting for a minister of light, but throwing Gerald into a counterfeit life.

"I don't hold it against God," he had told Cyrus. "I just wish I understood."

Gerald heard panting. He heard an animal approaching though he couldn't see it. He froze in anticipation of attack. Something jumped on him, knocking him over. It was licking his face. It was the dog! Cyrus must have let the dog out of the truck. It jumped on Gerald and he hugged it. Maybe Gerald didn't belong in the carnival. He couldn't even read a map. Maybe he could find his way back to Pierre. Gerald saw a falling fireball or streak of heat lightning in the cloudless night sky. He couldn't be sure, but he thought it was a lion flying through the sky with a trail of bees. He thought of his father in a place Gerald could not go because life was still in him. The Ghost Dancers also had been caught up beyond the sky and could not make themselves known. A wheel of their cars spun in the heavens, and a wheel above the wheel. The Milky Way was its exhaust trail. For a long time Gerald followed the wobbly sound of the convoy in the distance, then the sound was gone. The dog still trotted beside him. Maybe they would make it. Or maybe some of the voices Gerald heard were the ghosts of the Seventh Cavalry. Maybe the Wounded Knee Massacre continued, and he soon would be slaughtered in a world in danger of becoming a string of bones.

Acknowledgments

Porcupine's story is taken from James Mooney, *The Ghost-Dance Religion and the Sioux Outbreak of 1890* (University of Nebraska Press, 1991).

Kicking Bear's story is taken from James McLaughlin, *My Friend the Indian* (New York: Houghton Mifflin, 1910) and also appears in *Indian Oratory, Famous Speeches by Noted Indian Chieftains*, compiled by W. C. Vanderwerth (University of Oklahoma Press, 1971).

"James Mooney (Wasichu)" is taken from James Mooney, *The Ghost-Dance Religion and the Sioux Outbreak of 1890* (University of Nebraska Press, 1991) .

The Messiah letter is taken from the Arapaho version in James Mooney, *The Ghost-Dance Religion and the Sioux Outbreak of 1890* (University of Nebraska Press, 1991).

The first part of the statement of American Horse is taken from James Mooney, *The Ghost-Dance Religion and the Sioux Outbreak of 1890* (University of Nebraska Press, 1991).

The myth of Kurangwa is taken from James Mooney, *The Ghost-Dance Religion and the Sioux Outbreak of 1890* (University of Nebraska Press, 1991).

"The Ghost Dance at Wounded Knee" is taken from versions told by Dick Fool Bull at Rosebud Indian Reservation, South Dakota, 1967 and 1968, recorded by Richard Erdoes, in *American Indian Myths and Legends*, selected and edited by Richard Erdoes and Alfonso Ortiz, Pantheon Fairy Tale and Folklore Library (New York: Pantheon Books, 1984).

Acknowledgment to Jennifer Lynn Soule and Bradley Soule for their talk, "Death at the Hiawatha Asylum for Insane Indians," Center for Western Studies Dakota Conference, Augustana College, Sioux Falls, South Dakota, May 30, 2002.

After the conference, I stopped at the Hiawatha Asylum cemetery, which is on a dirt road a mile east of Canton, nine miles off I-29 on Highway 18, south of Sioux Falls. I left an offering of tobacco for the voices, none of which I heard, only imagined what they might have said, asking forgiveness for the trespass.

Some of the ideas for the spirits' songs in "A Time to Get In Gear" are from James Mooney, *The Ghost Dance Religion* (University of Nebraska Press, 1991).

Part 1 of Richard Cardinal's story in "A Green Rag-Braided Rug" is from "Alone and Very Scared," *Brandon Sun* newspaper, "Dimensions" section, Brandon, Manitoba, Canada, October 6, 1984.

Nuva' Ka Ro'rani'! is reprinted from James Mooney, *The Ghost Dance Religion* (University of Nebraska Press, 1991).

Acknowledgment for electronic publication to *Segue Online Literary Journal*, Miami University—Middletown, wwwmuohio.edu/segue/, November 2004, for "The Ghost Dance," "The Sioux Uprising," "Mankato Hanging," "Hiawatha Asylum for Insane Indians," "Auntie Opey," "A Time to Get In Gear," "Little Ghosts Running from Children," and "A Green Rag-Braided Rug."

A portion of "The Dance Partner" was read on September 19, 2004, on the Day to Day Program, National Public Radio, for the opening of the National Museum of the Native American in Washington, D.C.